ACTION ATLANTIC

U-BOAT SERIES BOOK TWO

EDWYN GRAY

WOLFPACK
PUBLISHING
— EST 2013 —

Action Atlantic
U-Boat Series Book Two
Edwyn Gray

Paperback Edition
© Copyright 2018 (as revised) Edwyn Gray

Wolfpack Publishing
6032 Wheat Penny Avenue
Las Vegas, NV 89122

ISBN: 978-1-64119-285-9

Library of Congress Control Number: 2018952544

For Sue and Mark

AUTHOR'S NOTES

The central characters in this story are wholly fictitious as indeed are most of the incidents. However this is a book about Germany's U-boats at war and for reasons of historical accuracy many of the subsidiary characters are real people.

Some fought and died for their country. Others survived the conflict and are happily still alive today. I wish to make it clear therefore that the words and actions ascribed to these real-life officers and men of the *Kriegsmarine* are entirely the product of my imagination and in no way necessarily reflect either their characters or their political views.

These men were dedicated professional seamen and true patriots. And although we found ourselves on opposing sides in 1939 I have a great admiration for their skills and a profound respect for their integrity. I hope they will understand and excuse my wilder flights of fancy.

Any attempt to recount the story of the U-boats at

war would be the poorer for their exclusion even though they only play fictitious roles in the combat career of *UB-44!*s skipper - *Kapitanleutnant* Bergman.

EDWYN GRAY

ACTION ATLANTIC

ONE

UB-44 dug her bows deeply into the mid-Atlantic swell as she headed east on the homeward leg of her sixth combat patrol. The grey hull, scarred by streaks of bright red rust where pounding seas had stripped the paint from her Krupp steel plating, creaked and groaned with the movement of the ocean, while an ungainly 5° starboard list - the result of faults in Numbers 2 and 5 bilge pumps, demonstrated the U- boats urgent need for overhaul and refitting on her return to Germany. *Kapitanleutnant* Konrad Bergman had made a routine request for dry-dock inspection in his Maintenance Report at the end of the fifth patrol but the operational demands of *BdU* had overridden all other considerations. And after a brief twenty-four-hour break to refuel, take on fresh torpedoes, and replenish stores, *UB-44* had been thrown back into battle.

This time, however, he was determined to have his boat properly checked by the dockyard experts even if it meant going direct to Rear Admiral Doenitz himself for permission. The U-boat war was quite dangerous enough

without the additional hazards of leaking plates and sluggish pumps.

It was the high summer of 1940. The clear skies and
blazing sun contrasted pleasantly with the blizzard conditions of their last operational mission inside the Arctic
Circle during the closing stages of the Norwegian
campaign and the men of the off-duty Watch sprawled
contentedly in the shade of the conning-tower enjoying
the warm fresh-tasting air. Some were dozing while others
exchanged dog-eared and much read letters from home. A
larger group, sitting in a circle around the U-boat's
105mm deck gun, were animatedly discussing how they
would spend their leave when *UB-44* got back to
Wilhelmshaven. All were relaxed and happy in the confident knowledge that the war was nearly over.

But, until the Peace Treaties were formally signed,
the reality of war remained and the duty lookouts, posted
to port and starboard of the bridge, scanned the horizon
with their powerful Zeiss binoculars vigilant and alert as
always for the first sign of danger. The conflict that had
begun when Hitler's Panzers crossed the Polish border on
1st September 1939 might be nearly over but, with the
ferocity of cornered animals, the British still had the
ability to hit hard. And it didn't pay to relax precautions
when travelling on the surface in areas covered by RAF
Coastal Command's ubiquitous flying-boats.

The Iron Cross emblem blazoned high up on the side
of *UB-44's* conning-tower indicated that she was a
member of the famed 10th Flotilla while a line of white
symbols painted below and to the left of the flotilla
insignia proudly proclaimed the history of the U-boat's
career as a raider of the deep.

Two aircraft silhouettes, a Blenheim bomber shot

down during the first week of the war and a Fairy Sword-fish snapped up off Narvik on their fifth patrol, demonstrated *UB-44*'s willingness to remain on the surface and fight it out — while a group of five white oblong bars recorded her tally of enemy merchantmen sunk. Proof, if any was needed, of her skipper's prowess as a commerce raider. And below, in pride of place, a few fluent strokes of paint brush had captured the outline of a British cruiser to boast their most famous success to date — the sinking of HMS *Salisbury*

Sanitatsobermaat Hans Steiner, *UB-44*'s medical orderly and unofficial war artist, carefully added a sixth white oblong to mark the destruction of the tanker they had torpedoed the previous night, wiped his brush on the cloth tied to his wrist, and screwed the top back on his paint bottle. Then, leaning back critically, he checked that the proportions were correct and that the fresh new symbol was in line with its five weather-worn companions.

'Watch it, Hans, you'll be over the side if you go back any further. Come over here and grab a drink.'

Steiner stepped gingerly over the sleeping forms resting against the base of the conning-tower and joined the circle of men grouped around the deck gun.

'Wetting the baby's head?' he asked Willi Schmidt, a fresh-faced young man who seemed to be leading the celebrations.

'Who knows?' Schmidt shrugged. 'Gerda was eight months through her time when we left Wilhelmshaven so it's always possible. That's the worst of the U-boat service. No news from home until you get back to base.'

'Well *you* volunteered for it, Willi,' Brunner pointed out. 'So it's no good griping. You should have hung on to that job of yours in the Hamburg shipyards. Christ! Fancy giving up a job that exempts you from being conscripted and then coming to serve in one of these bloody iron coffins.'

'I suppose you'd have stayed at home if they'd given you half the chance,' Schmidt bit back.

'You bet I would,' grinned Brunner. 'Just think of it. All you loving husbands away at sea and all those lonely wives wanting a bit of comfort. I'd have screwed my bloody balls off given half the chance.'

'If you had any,' someone taunted.

Brunner retaliated good-humouredly with a wild sweep of his massive arms but the culprit ducked and he tangled with Mareau the brawny ex-miner from Alsace who was sitting next in line. Roaring like a bull he dived at his attacker and, within seconds, everyone else had joined in the exuberant rough-and-tumble.

Looking down from his lofty perch on top of the conning- tower *Kapitanleutnant* Bergman heard the laughter and the corners of his mouth turned up as he watched the men enjoying themselves. He wished that he could have shared their carefree gaiety. But the burning heat of the noonday sun reminded him of *UB-44's* fateful mission to the Gulf of Mexico in January 1940. And the memory of what he had done sent a cold shiver down his spine. The tormenting guilt left by the incident had faded with the passing of time but even now, after six months, the doubts remained. And the fact that he had acted on the direct orders of the Fuehrer did nothing to ease his conscience. Bergman's only consolation lay in the fact that the U-boat's crew had no knowledge of the crime they had helped to commit. And for their sakes he was glad.

Oberbootsmann Herzog, *UB-44's* coxswain and senior warrant officer, and a veteran whose U-boat service stretched back to the days of World War I, heaved himself up through the narrow circle of the conning-tower hatch, drew a deep breath of clean salt air into his lungs, and made his way over to the starboard side of the *wintergarten* - the 20mm gun platform abaft the bridge. Resting his elbows on the rails he stared down at the sea swirling past the ballast tanks as the U-boat's bows cut through the water at a steady 15 knots. The sea was transparently clear and he could see the curving plates of the starboard tank deep beneath the surface slicing through the water like a vast aquatic animal playfully running abreast of the submarine.

But Herzog was unmoved. His thoughts were elsewhere. He spat into the sea carefully and deliberately. Three patrols - and that bastard Bergman was still alive. So be it. But enjoy the sweet smell of victory while you can, *Herr Kapitanleutnant* because it won't last forever. And if *I* don't get you I'll see that *someone* does. No doubt the Gestapo would be interested in an officer of the *Kriegsmarine* who kept a Jewish mistress. Herzog grinned to himself. He must remember to make a discreet telephone call when they got back to Wilhelmshaven.

He stuck a cigarette in his mouth, cupped his hands to the match, and dragged a mouthful of smoke into his lungs. *Koenig* had gone and, with her, a thousand of Germany's finest sailors. And Herzog was the only man aboard who knew that Bergman was responsible for her destruction. He threw the cigarette into the sea with a gesture of disgust. If he didn't seize his chance now, before the war fizzled out, he might never get another.

And it would be a pity to waste the skipper on the Gestapo. The question was ... how?

Leutnant zur See Hermann Bauer, *UB-44's* Executive Officer, joined the captain on the bridge as the sharp tinkle of eight bells signalled the end of the Forenoon Watch. 'Seems quiet enough, sir,' he observed. 'Any news?' 'Nothing so far, Number One. Don't worry, we'll hear soon enough. But until we do I want full alert maintained - the men are already beginning to take it easy.' He nodded in the direction of the sailors enjoying the sun on the foredeck. 'I hadn't the heart to keep them below in this sort of weather. But it's a bloody silly risk to take in enemy waters.'

'But surely it's all over bar the shouting?' Bauer asked. 'We occupy the western coast of Europe from the North Cape to the Pyrenees, France has surrendered, and I've even heard rumours that we've taken over the Channel Islands. I don't see how the war can last much longer. The British haven't a hope in hell of beating us now.'

'Perhaps not, Bauer,' Bergman observed drily, 'but, on the other hand, *we* haven't beaten *them* yet either. Remember Clausewitz - those lectures at the Academy? Never underestimate an enemy. It's the biggest mistake you can make.'

'I'm not underestimating them, sir. I'm being realistic. They might have saved half their army at Dunkirk but they lost all their weapons and tanks. And it's not much use trying to fight a Panzer Division with a pitch-fork.'

'You may be right. But remember - if you can stick the pitch-fork into the driver's belly even the best and biggest Panzer tank will just go round in circles.'

Meister, *UB-44s* senior radio operator, heaved himself

half out of the upper conning-tower hatch, his pallid face flushed with excitement.

'Special wireless announcement just coming through from Berlin on 4995kc/s, sir. Shall I relay it over the loud-speaker system?'

Bergman squatted down beside the hatch and kept his voice low. 'What's it about?'

'The Fuehrer has been making an important speech to the *Reichstag,* sir. I think he's made some sort of peace offer.' 'Any details?'

'No, sir. But they've just begun putting out a recording of the full speech on Berlin Radio and *BdU* is relaying it on the signal band.'

Bergman thought for a moment. He preferred to censor all news items before they reached the men - some of the wilder propaganda broadcasts were so palpably false that they were beginning to undermine morale. But, on the other hand, the rumours of peace were getting too frequent *and* far too convincing. And with the scent of victory in the air it did not take much to blunt the sharp edges of the crew's alertness. Perhaps on balance it might help. And obviously *BdU* intended them to hear it. He nodded his approval.

'Very well, Meister, you may relay it over the loud-speakers. But keep the volume down — I don't want the men on Duty Watch distracted.'

Funkobermaat Meister slid back down the conning-tower ladder with the practiced ease of a comedian falling down a man-hole in an old silent movie and, moments later, Bergman heard the metallic click of the master switch echo in the bridge loudspeaker as the U-boat's radio was linked into the internal communications system. The harsh arrogance of the Fuehrer's voice was instantly recognized and the men relaxing on deck roused themselves to listen. Even the high-spirited group clustered around the gun clambered to their feet and drew closer to the conning-tower so that they could hear better.

As he watched their rapt expressions Bergman felt a strange fear in his heart. What was it that gave this man such power over Germany? Every time he saw the effect of Hitler's words on his listeners he experienced the same uneasy feeling in the pit of his stomach. He could still remember the magnetic influence those rhetorical phrases had exerted over his own immature mind when he was still a young man. But, as he had seen through the shabby sham and discovered the evils that lay at the foundation of the Nazi creed, he had grown to hate the voice - and the man - who now controlled his beloved Germany. And he had not forgotten that his attack on the *Koenig* had been carried out on express orders from the Fuehrer. Perhaps Rahel had been right. Perhaps there were occasions when orders should not be obeyed. But it was too late for regrets now. *Koenig* had gone and in her destruction he had become a mass murderer.

'Pay attention to your duties, Schrieber!'

Bergman's voice had a sharp edge to it as he saw the starboard sky lookout turning his head slightly to one side so that he could hear the Fuehrer's words more clearly. Schrieber stiffened obediently, grasped his Zeiss binoculars a fraction tighter, and continued his relentless search of the empty sky. That's the trouble with the skipper, he grumbled to himself. He doesn't want peace. He's only happy when there's a bloody war going on.

But the magnetic, almost hypnotic, effect of Hitler's voice was something that not even Bergman's iron discipline could withstand and he knew that Schrieber, like every other man on *UB-44.* was listening with rapt attention. And despite everything, the *Kapitanleutnant* found himself doing the same.

'... If this struggle continues it can only end in the annihilation of one of us. Mr. Churchill thinks it will be Germany. I know it will be Britain. I am not the vanquished begging for mercy. I speak as a victor. I see no reason why this war must go on. We should like to avert the sacrifices that must claim millions.. .'

'Turn it off, Meister,' Bergman called down the voice-pipe that linked the bridge to the radio office abaft the control room. 'And switch me into the system.'

He swung open the small grey door of the watertight cabinet, pulled out the hand microphone, and waited until the green light flashed to show he was connected to the loudspeaker system. He pushed down the 'speak' button with his thumb.

'This is the Captain. You have been listening to the Fuehrer and now I want you to listen to me. This speech was only a peace offer to the British - it does not mean that the war is over. Any relaxation on your part at this particular time could lead to disaster. Most of you have served with me for almost a year now and you are well aware that the first thought in my mind at all times is your safety and the safety of *UB-44.* Once you relax your vigilance and you put your own and your comrade's lives at risk. I will not let that happen. So hear this. Any man who slacks, any man who passes on rumours, will have to answer to me. Until the war is officially over we must all remain instantly ready for action. Remember what the Fuehrer said — we are the victors. But that does not mean we can be complacent. Our troops occupy Brussels and Paris but they are not yet in

London. And, until they are, and until Britain has surrendered, we must continue our struggle in defence of the Fatherland. That is all.'

Bergman's lips curled in self-disgust at his hypocrisy. Even if Churchill surrendered - and somehow he thought it unlikely - the war would go on. There would be new nations to conquer and fresh continents on which to impose the Nazi's vaunted New Order. Rahel and her friends were right. Hitler was mad and his appetite for power would not be satisfied until he had devoured the entire world. And the fighting would go on until, inevitably, Germany was shattered, exhausted, and defeated. It would be a very long time before the men of *UB-44* returned to their homes in peace - if they survived that long. But what could he, an insignificant U-boat commander, do about such things?

'Aircraft! Starboard 90!'

Torn from his reverie Bergman snatched the glasses to his eyes and scanned the sector of sky identified by Schrieber. A few wisps of cirrus cloud, sign-posting the depression forecast by Hauptmann's meteorological report an hour earlier, hung like lonely puffs of cotton wool in the northern sky and, 10,000 feet beneath them, he could see the sinister black dot of an approaching aircraft. Too distant to identify, yet close enough to take no chances.

'Diving stations!'

He thumbed the klaxon alarm and its rasping squawk brought every man to his feet in an instant. Even Herzog, deep in his dark schemes on the rails of the gun platform, came to life. Vaulting to the deck with an agility that belied his heavy body he dragged open the door leading into the lower conning-tower and propelled the men inside with an ungentle thrust while the strident bark of his voice shouted the rest into a disciplined line.

Essen, *UB-44*'s warrant gunner, was in the control room when the alarm sounded and, appreciating the danger of the situation, he hurried up the ladder to assist the Coxswain. Kneeling over the lower hatch, he caught the men as Herzog pushed them into the compartment, and guided them down the ladder into the control room below.

'Next one coming!'

'Right... down you go, lad. Hatch clear!'

'Next man forward ...'

Brunner, the genial giant who acted as *UB-44's* wardroom steward, swore loudly as Aachan, the next in line, missed his footing on the narrow steel rungs and trod heavily on his fingers. But the mishap had no effect on his rate of descent. Plenty of time to tell Aachan what he thought of him later. Right now all that mattered was getting clear of the ladder. And until the lower hatch was clear, none of the Duty Watch on the bridge could start coming down.

For the first time in his career Bergman knew he had been caught with his pants down. Thank God the enemy aircraft was only a lumbering, slow-moving Sunderland flying-boat. Why the hell had he allowed so many men to come up on deck? He'd been berating everyone for relaxing and thinking the war was over, yet, for sheer bloody complacency, he'd been the biggest culprit of all.

Even allowing only an extra five seconds for each man to squeeze down through the hatch and drop into the control room at least a minute was added to the U-boat's crucial diving time. He waited impatiently for the deck to clear. A Sunderland's maximum operational speed was

210 knots. That meant the flying-boat would be closing the gap by about... he did a quick mental calculation ... three miles every minute of elapsed time. She must be eight or nine miles away at present. Another minute and she'd be down to five. And it would take at least a further minute before *UB- 44's* crew could start their normal diving routine. It was going to be bloody close!

Down below, in the control room, the men of the Duty Watch sweated to get the U-boat under the sea. And, in the engine-room, *Obermaschinist* Kohr pushed the 2,800 hp MAN diesels to full power in response to the telegraph. Maximum thrust was needed from the propellors to force the U-boat down when the hydroplanes tilted into the diving position. And it was that impetus of speed that was vital for, at any moment, he would get the order: 'clutches out — switches on' and then the throbbing oil engines would be immediately cut off before they sucked every cubic inch of air out of the U-boat's interior as the intakes were sealed off.

It was a tricky decision to time in an emergency. The electric motors could not produce enough thrust and it was essential to maintain diesel power to the very last moment. As he crouched over the controls Kohr was glad that the decision didn't rest with him.

Bauer had left the bridge at the first warning squawk of the klaxon and he was already in the control room supervising the diving routine. He cocked an eye at Neisser, the Second Coxswain, standing at the foot of the ladder.

'How many more?'

'Only four, sir. Plus Herzog, Essen, .and the Duty Watch.'

Bergman slid down into the lower compartment,

thrust the men aside, and pushed his head inside the opened hatch. His voice sounded oddly hollow as it echoed back from the steel walls.

'Take her down, Number One! I'll get this lot inside - don't worry. I'll see that we make it.'

Bauer nodded as Bergman shoved the next man down the ladder before turning to climb back up to the bridge.

'Open main vents! Flood all tanks! 'planes hard a'dive!'

There was a muffled roar as the sea hammered into the empty ballast tanks and Bauer felt *UB-44* tilting forward

'All men accounted for, sir.'

'Good. Stand by for the Duty Watch.' Bauer glanced at his watch. Ninety-three seconds. He shrugged. It could have been worse. The men on deck had been mostly stokers and mechanics, and they weren't used to getting below at the double. They hadn't done so badly in the circumstances. The enemy flying-boat must be about five miles away by now - and that meant he had only a minute or so left to get *UB-44* safely below the surface so that she could glide down into the green depths of the ocean and escape her attacker.

The Duty lookouts slid expertly down the ladder and landed with a series of heavy thuds on the steel plating at the bottom. They ducked quickly through the forward watertight door into the crew's quarter so that the control-room was not cluttered with unnecessary bodies. Bauer glanced up at the indicators and watched the long red needles inching down. Ten feet already. If the skipper didn't hurry he'd have to swim for it.

Flying Officer Maitland stared down intently at the

mirrored surface of the sea as Sunderland No F-9427 settled into her stately approach run.

'She seems to be diving, skipper. Think we'll nail her?'

'I wouldn't like to bet on it, Toby. If we were carrying depth-charges we might stand a chance but as we've only got bombs it means we'll have to get a direct hit to do any good.'

He clipped the bottom section of his face mask into position to bring the microphone closer to his mouth. 'Got her in the sights yet, Brown?'

Stretched out on his stomach in the cramped bomb-aimers position below the nose gun turret Flight Sergeant Brown squinted through the sights.

'Not yet, skipper,' he reported through the intercom. 'I can see the bastard large and clear but he's not on the line so far. Can you come in from astern about 20° starboard?'

'Do my best, bombardier, but I can see sweet fanny up here. And I don't want to lose ground speed. Toby, can you give me a course?'

Maitland pressed his face up against the screen. The cockpit position was situated high up on the huge flared hull and it was difficult to see anything directly beneath the flight path.

'Try zero-six-five.'

The flying-boat tilted its wings and the four Bristol Pegasus Mk XXII engines screamed to full power as Murray rammed the throttles open.

'What the hell's she hanging about for?'

'God knows! Must have caught her napping in the sun... I wonder if it's the same U-boat that sent that tanker up in flames last night?'

Maitland's eyes narrowed as he recalled the smouldering wreck they had sighted a few hours earlier. The blackened flame-seared superstructure. The burned out lifeboats. And the lifeless bodies floating face down in the thick oil sludge that polluted the sea for half a mile around the U-boat's victim.

'I hope so,' he said quietly. 'I'd like to give the bastard a taste of his own medicine.'

'Sights on!'

'Okay. Steady at 0-6-5. Ground speed 190. It's all yours.'

Bergman glanced up as the Sunderland came in for the kill. *UB-44's* bows were well down under the surface and he could hear the sea rushing into the ballast tanks forcing her deeper with every second. Only the conning-tower remained above water and a wall of spray crashed upwards as the sea surged against the curved steel base. Herzog was standing on the ladder with only the upper part of his body visible. The hatch cover was raised at right angles ready for closing and he was supporting it with one hand as if waiting for the skipper to take the weight while he slid below to the control room.

'Everyone down, Chief?'

'No, sir. Raulheim's still missing.'

Bergman cursed and cast an anxious eye at the sky again. The Sunderland had turned and was coming in from astern - about three miles away and descending with the slow dignity of a stately Duchess coming down a flight of marble stairs. It was lucky that flying-boats weren't built for dive-bombing.

'Where the hell is he?'

'Not sure, sir. tie was on the foredeck last time I saw him.'

UB-44 was running awash. Only six feet of conning-tower still showed above the surface and she was diving steeply at 10 knots. A continuous wall of water cascaded over the bulwarks of the bridge as Bergman groped his way forward through the spray.

'Get below, Chief!' he yelled. 'I'll just take a quick look to make sure he isn't caught up on something.'

It was worse than being exposed to the fury of a monsoon rain-storm and Bergman was drenched to the skin by the time he had clawed his way to the forward end of the bridge. The whip-sharp spray lashed his face as he stared down over the rim of the conning-tower. But there was nothing to see - only the angry sea tearing itself into a lathering froth as it smashed against the half-submerged deck gun. If Raulheim was trapped in that cauldron Bergman didn't give much for his chances of survival. He shrugged.

UB-44's commander was no sentimentalist; and he had lost men before. And on this occasion that fool Raulheim only had himself to blame for not moving quickly enough when he heard the alarm. Bergman turned away reluctantly as he forced himself to abandon the search.

The roar of the flying-boat's four engines rose full-throated above the tumultuous noise of the sea. The Sunderland was barely a mile away and closing fast. At any moment the bomb racks would slide out from under the wing roots, someone would pull a lever, the clamps would open, and the bombs would screech down on their target. Raulheim must be sacrificed. There could be no alternative. Thrusting himself away from the bridge screen Bergman clambered back towards the hatch. His body bent under the weight of water pouring over the conning-tower and, holding an arm up to protect his face from the angry sea, he groped like a blind man searching for a familiar door.

Another fifteen seconds and the entire conning-tower would be under the surface. The sea, pouring down through the open hatch, would seal the fate of the U-boat as surely and effectively as a direct hit from one of the Sunderland's bombs. Reaching the hatch Bergman fell on his knees. The sea swirled wildly across the steel-plated deck, snatching at his legs as it tried to drag him away. He swore and stretched his arm into the spray as he felt for the hatch cover. But his hands were clawing at thin air. *The heavy steel hatch cover was firmly shut.*

Hammering the cover with his fist he waited for it to be opened. The possibility that something was wrong did not even cross his mind. And despite his impatience he assumed that Herzog had taken the sensible and elementary precaution of closing the hatch to prevent the sea from flooding in. It would have been the typical reaction of a veteran U- boat sailor - keep the inside of the boat dry at all costs.

But when Bergman found the knocking brought no response he felt a bead of cold sweat trickle down his back. Seized by panic he beat a frenzied tattoo on the hatch cover again. Nothing happened. The sea began creeping over the lower edges of the conning-tower and he was suddenly thrown, slithering and sliding on the wet deck, back towards the bows as *UB-44* increased her angle of descent.

Someone had pushed the hydroplanes over to full tilt in a last frantic effort to get the U-boat beneath the surface before the bombs crashed down. The sharp tilting movement brought an unexpected, if momentary, reprieve. With the sides of the conning-tower lifted clear of the surface the sea ceased to spill over the lip of the coaming. But the deluge of spray grew in intensity and Bergman found himself crawling uphill on his hands and knees as he tried to reach the hatch again - struggling against the weight of water flooding back down the slope as the escaping sea surged through the drainage holes cut into the steel sides at deck level.

Kneeling over the tightly clamped hatch cover he beat at it with his fists until he was almost sobbing with exhaustion. 'For Christ's sake - open up! Open the bloody hatch you stupid bastards!'

But the noise of the sea - roaring defiantly as *UB-44* thrust its barnacled rust-streaked body into the ocean's virginal womb - drowned Bergman's screams. And the men huddled in the bright warmth of the control room beneath his feet heard nothing.

TWO

'There's someone still on deck, skipper,' Maitland yelled into Murray's ear as the flying-boat lumbered down towards her target.

'The first of the rats leaving the sinking ship, I shouldn't wonder,' Murray grinned. 'How much longer, bombardier?'

Brown's voice was tense with excitement. 'Twenty seconds, sir. Hold the old girl steady and we've got the bastard stone cold.'

Murray's hands tightened on the controls. He could feel the entire structure of the flying-boat shuddering with strain as the engines peaked at maximum power. He felt sure they were over the limit. But he had sense enough not to look at the instruments. No time to think of safety when their first kill was imminent.

'Toby - keep a weather eye on that character on the bridge. Just in case he starts waving a white flag. I wouldn't mind capturing a U-boat in full working order. One up over the Navy, eh?'

Fifteen fourteen ... thirteen ... Bergman's moment of

hysteria quickly evaporated with the knowledge that he was trapped. Staring down at the hatch cover he checked the angle of the lever operating the clamps inside. It was locked hard over. Some stupid bastard had fastened the clips. That meant there was no hope of prising the heavy counterweighted lid open even supposing he had a suitable tool at hand to do it with. And, if the correct diving routine had been observed, the lower hatch would be securely clipped as well. No wonder his frantic hammering had not been heard by the men inside the U-boat.

But there was still one last chance. Stumbling forward he wrenched the cover off the bridge telephone and reached for the hand-piece. Whether Bauer would risk bringing *UB-* 44 to the surface was anybody's guess — but it was worth a try. As his fingers touched the telephone the agonized expression on Werth's face suddenly flashed before his eyes and he recalled his own ruthless decision to abandon the wounded man when *UB-44* was under air attack in the Schillig Roads.[1] What was the phrase in that English book he had read at school: do-as-you-would-be-done-by. The corners of his mouth turned down at the bitter irony of the situation.

Grasping the telephone he lifted it from its cradle. But it never reached his ear. There was a sudden triumphant crash of water as the sea enveloped the conning-tower and a rush of solid water struck him with the force of a bomb-blast. The instrument was ripped from his hand as the sea threw him back against the steel side of the conning-tower with a strength that knocked the breath from his body. Water raged and thundered down upon him from all directions, beating him to his knees, bruising his body, and lashing his flesh like a thousand ice-cold scourges. Fighting his way to his feet and sobbing for breath the *Kapitanleutnant* staggered forward groping blindly for the steel tubes of the periscope standards.

The sea swirled up his legs as *UB-44* slid deeper beneath the surface and, instinctively, he tore off his sea boots. Gasping and choking, the salt water burning his eyes and clogging his nose, Bergman grabbed for the periscope and dragged himself upwards like a man climbing a tall tree to escape from a flood. Even the greased pole that had featured in many a Fleet Regatta when he had been a cadet was child's play by comparison. His hands, cut and bleeding, slipped helplessly on the smooth metal but by sheer willpower he hauled himself inch by inch up the narrow steel tube. And the fact that the periscope was sinking beneath the surface almost as fast as he was climbing it only added a further nightmare quality to his ordeal.

As his head broke clear of the surface Bergman shook the water from his ears and gulped mouthfuls of air into his lungs. Then, clinging tightly to the steel pole, he tried to think. But the respite was only momentary. *UB-44* *continued* plunging downwards and it was obvious that Bauer intended to take her well below periscope depth so that the sea would act as a protective shield against the bombs.

The bombs! Good God! - he'd forgotten about the flying- boat. Raising his head he looked upward in time to see the first two bombs dropping lazily away from their racks under the Sunderland's wings.

Suddenly all thoughts of personal survival were overwhelmed by the primitive instincts that bound him to his boat and his men.

'Get her down, Bauer! Faster, man. *Faster!*'

Locked inside their iron coffin the crew were deaf to his shouts. And Bergman knew it. But it was impossible to witness *UB-44's* destruction without trying to give them some sort of warning and the commands sprang to his lips before he realized the futility of his efforts.

As if responding to the orders of its commander the U- boat lurched deeper and the tip of the periscope slipped beneath the surface in a whisper of spray. Bergman released his grip on the steel tube and his arms clawed at the water in an effort to swim clear of the powerful suction created by the submerging submarine. He had just sufficient time to gulp one last mouthful of air into his lungs before he, too, was pulled down into the swirling vortex.

Five feet... ten feet... twenty feet...

The blood pounded in his ears as he was dragged down, and despite the strength in his muscles he seemed impotent to overcome the invisible forces drawing him into the depths. He kicked and fought to escape but the frantic struggle only weakened his fast ebbing strength further. A strange lethargy filled his limbs with lead and, yielding to the inevitable, he allowed himself to be sucked deeper... *CRUM-M-P! CRUM-M-P!*

An angry mule kicked Bergman in the chest as the shock wave of the exploding bombs struck his body. The pressure created by the concussion threatened to burst his ear-drums and he wanted to scream out with the agonizing pain. Instinctively fighting for survival Bergman kept his mouth tightly clamped but not even his iron will-power could contain the agony in his tortured lungs A trickle of air bubbles dribbled from his lips and climbed towards the surface. And through the swirling mists of unconsciousness he was dimly aware that he was floating upwards as well. Clinging to the last dregs of air in his lungs he kicked hard with his legs ..._

A sudden deafening roar replaced the pounding sensation in his ears and the intensity of the noise forced a scream from his lips. But the shriek of pain told Bergman he was still alive. His mouth was open and the sea was not pouring down his throat!

Rolling on to his back he gazed at the azure blue sky and the golden disc of the sun. The Sunderland was climbing and circling for a second bombing run and he realized that it had been the roar of her engines as she skimmed the surface with throttles wide open that had struck his ears when he first broke into the warm daylight. He looked around.

The sea was calm with only a gentle swell disturbing the smooth surface. There was no slick of oil, no wreckage, no gushing bubbles of air to pin-point the grave of the shattered U-boat. So Bauer and *UB-44* were safe too. Thank God for that. A sitting target and the British had missed. Bergman paddled gently with his feet as he regained his breath. Ironically he could thank the Royal Air Force for his survival. The force of the bomb explosions must have thrown him beyond the deadly grip of the U-boat's suction and allowed him to float safely to the surface.

So the bombs had saved him. But, for what? There was no lifebelt and no life-raft. He was alone on his own - an insignificant solitary spot on the vast surface of the Atlantic Ocean. How long could he last out before his strength finally gave out - fifteen minutes? Perhaps thirty. Certainly no more. And, in the end, death was inevitable. He would sink down slowly under the sea until the water gurgled into his nose and mouth forcing one last super-human effort to survive. Then his arms would rise up and he would slide under again — for ever.

His thoughts began to wander. He thought of his father's death in *UC-115* in 1918. Perhaps he was lucky. Better to drown cleanly than to die, choking and gasping for breath like the men of *UC-115,* trapped in the gas poisoned hull of a sunken submarine. Much better.

'Did we get it, Toby?' Murray asked anxiously as he threw the flying-boat into a tight circling climb.

His co-pilot peered through the perspex windows of the cockpit canopy. The exploding bombs had left two spreading circular patches of agitated water that still seethed and bubbled like milk simmering in a saucepan.

'Looks like it got away, damn it! No sign of oil on the surface and there's no air bubbles.' Maitland widened his search area beyond the two angry white circles that scarred the sea. 'Wait a minute. I can see something - star-board of the nearest bomb pattern.'

Murray tilted the Sunderland on to its right wing tip and circled the spot.

'It's a body, sir,' Brown reported from his uncomfort-able perch beneath the bow turret. 'Seems to be alive - the poor bastard's trying to swim.'

'Must be the one we saw on deck when it dived,' Maitland suggested. 'Got himself marooned topsides and then washed overboard when they submerged.'

The pilot shook his head.

'I know U-boat captains are a callous bunch but I can't see them abandoning one of their men like that. They might be Germans but they're still human, you know.' He centered the control column to bring the flying-boat level and began throttling back. 'I'd say those bombs we dropped have burst the hull and he's the only one to get out alive.'

'But surely there'd be oil on the surface - and more bodies,' Maitland objected. 'I grant you we've chalked up a "possible" but Intelligence won't let you get away with a "probable" on that sort of evidence.'

Murray pushed the stick forward as he aimed the Sunderland towards the sea. 'They'd do even better than that - if we brought home a prisoner.'

His right hand eased the throttle controls back further as he peered out through the side window of the cockpit.

'What do you reckon for wind direction, Toby?'

Maitland stared down at the sea trying to judge the answer by the lazy drift of the surface swell. 'I'd say dead ahead, sir. And not more than 5 knots

'That's what I figured too. Hang on tight, chaps. We're going down.'

The sharp keel of the Sunderland's lower hull kissed the surface like a skater skimming the ice and Murray balanced the heavy flying-boat with the delicacy of a jeweler weighing diamonds as his hands felt for the wind direction through the movements of the controls. The Sunderland whispered upwards for a few moments and then sat down hard with a thud that made the fuselage creak. A giant wash rose wing high on each beam but the aircraft maintained a level balance and both floats settled into the sea simultaneously.

Once safely on the surface Murray throttled back sharply and the Sunderland, slowing to 60 knots, lost way rapidly. Transformed from a graceful bird to an ungainly four-engined motor boat it slewed to port and began to taxi slowly towards the object rising and falling gently in the swell.

'Toby, get down to the midship's hatch with Brown. Fasten a line to the dinghy and sling it out. I'll try and tow it downwind so that he can grab it. But you two stay inside the plane. Understood? I don't want anyone left behind if we have to take off in a hurry.'

Bergman's feelings were mixed as he watched the Sunderland touch down on the sea. His first reaction was one of instinctive fear that they intended to machine-gun him in the water and, in sudden panic, he had ducked under the surface to escape the bullets. But, when he emerged choking and gasping for breath almost a minute later, he remembered what Otto Kretschmer had told him while he was still under training before the war: *The British fight hard - but fair. Make sure you do the same.*

Kretschmer, now captain of *U-gg* and one of Germany's top aces, had practised what he preached. And Bergman had tried to do the same himself. Despite the lies pumped out by the Nazi propaganda machine he knew that the enemy had fought a clean war. And machine-gunning survivors was something that just did not happen - and that was true of both sides. He felt suddenly ashamed of his fears.

It was ironic that Bauer's prophecy should come true so quickly. The war *was* nearly over - at least, so far as he was concerned. Bergman's arms paddled lazily as he waited. Now it would be a matter of warm dry clothes, a searching interrogation by Admiralty Intelligence officers, and then a prison camp somewhere in England. Probably, some time later, a free trip to Canada at the enemy's expense where he had heard the British were setting up special camps for U- boat crews. Well it might have been worse. At least he was still alive.

Rolling over on to his back he trod water and watched

the Sunderland taxi across the surface. It reminded him of a skier coming to a halt in a slither of ice spray and scattered white snow on the slopes of the Grunnenberg, the mountain that brooded menacingly over his home in Vintenschloss. Bergman wondered how long it would be before he saw Bavaria again. Or before he found Rahel - if she had not already disappeared for ever in the course of her cat-and- mouse pursuit by the Gestapo. If Bauer was right it would only be a matter of weeks or, at most, months. But if his own pessimistic forebodings were correct it could be years. And by then Germany would probably be no more than a pile of bomb-shattered rubble.

The flying-boat taxied towards him and, accepting the inevitable, Bergman raised an arm out of the water to make sure they could see him. The midship's hatch just abaft the wing-roots was opened from inside and, as he watched, a small yellow package was tossed out. It burst open on striking the water and Bergman saw that it was an inflatable dinghy similar to the *flaschesboot* carried by *UB-44*.

The yellow dinghy drifted down-wind on the end of a line but Bergman's rising optimism plunged to despair as he gauged the distance. He had barely enough strength left to float, and a swim of several hundred yards was out of the question in his exhausted condition. Surely, having survived his previous ordeal, fate would not allow him to drown with rescue so close at hand.

The propellers of the Sunderland's two inboard engines began spinning faster and the flying-boat moved gently down-wind pulling the dinghy with it. As the speed increased the yellow raft streamed away from the hull until it was being towed at an angle of 45°. Murray knew his job and he guided the dinghy with the skill of a man jockeying a kite into the air against the wind. Bergman could appreciate the pilot's seamanship as the dinghy swept behind him like a paravane picking up the mooring rope of a mine. There was no need to swim. All he had to do was to reach up and grasp the line as it passed over his head.

He grabbed with both hands. The thin cord cut the salt- burned flesh of his palms but he was past caring about pain. The dinghy was a bare ten yards away and he clung grimly to the rope as Murray turned the flying-boat to starboard to draw it towards the U-boat captain. Bergman threw his arms over the bulging rubber sides of the flimsy craft as it bumped against his chest and dragged himself aboard. Then, exhausted by the effort, he tumbled into the bobbing dinghy and collapsed in a heap on its taut fabric floor.

Leutnant z.s. Hermann Bauer had begun shouting his orders while he was still sliding down the narrow steel ladder into the control room. The klaxon alarm had already sent the Duty Watch scurrying to their stations and it was standard procedure for the Executive Officer to start the intricate diving drill while the Commander was still on deck. It saved valuable seconds and the U-boat was usually half-way through its submergence routine by the time the hatches were secure and the skipper was safely down in the control- room.

'Open main vents! Flood all tanks! Stand by engine and motors.'

The big wheels controlling the Kingston valves spun rapidly from right to left and the sea surged hungrily into the empty tanks. Within thirty seconds the U-boat would have lost its positive buoyancy as the growing weight of water ballast in the tanks destroyed its minutely balanced trim. Then, aided by the angle of the flipper-like hydroplanes at bow and stern, the propellers would thrust her under the sea. And, if the drill was executed efficiently, sixty seconds after the alarm squawked its first strident warning, *UB-44* would be sinking safely beneath the surface into her rightful domain - the silent green depths of the underwater world.

'Stop engines!'

Leutnant (*Ing*) Veitch, crouched at his control panel in the cramped cavern of the engine room, heard the order and killed the MAN diesels with the flick of a finger.

'Engines stopped. Clutches out. Close exhaust vent and induction valve.'

Obermaschinist Paul Kohn reached up and pulled the lever of the baffle. It slid down smoothly and there was a muffled clang of metal somewhere high above his head. Then, turning slightly to his left, he grasped the valve wheel and spun it clockwise.

Bauer waited until the green light flickered to indicate that the high induction valve was closed off and sealed. He could still remember the lecture at the Periscope School which had dealt at gruesome length with the causes of various submarine disasters. And for some reason the loss of the USS *Squalus* in May 1939 had stuck in memory with uncanny vividness. The American submarine had gone down off the New England coast with the loss of more than half her crew because the high induction valve had failed to close correctly. And he had a fetish for checking this particular operation more than any other.

Perhaps it was because the shutting of the valve was not done in his presence. In the US Navy the hydraulic control was situated in the control room under the eyes of the Watch Officer. But in an operational U-boat the vital valve wheel was operated behind the watertight doors leading to the engine-room and there was only the green light on the Diving Indicator Panel to confirm that the gaping mouth of the valve, situated on deck just aft of the conning-tower, was firmly shut and secured.

'Upper hatch closed! Clips on.'

The shouted report bounced and echoed around the bare steel walls of the lower conning-tower compartment robbing it of all personal identity. Closing the hatch was the captain's job. And it fastened the final seal. *UB-44* was now completely watertight with every vent, aperture, hatch, and valve tightly shut down except for the open flooding valves admitting the sea into the ballast tanks that were slung, saddle-like, on either side of the narrow circular hull.

A pair of grubby sea boots emerged through the lower hatch set in the arched steel roof of the control room and, moments later, Herzog's head ducked down through the circular opening.

'The skipper says to hurry up, sir,' he gasped breathlessly. 'The enemy aircraft has just started its bombing run.'

Bauer obeyed instantly and without question. 'Switches on — group up. Full ahead both. Planes down - maximum angle. Hold and trim at 50 feet.'

The hum of the electric motors whined to a higher pitch and Bauer could feel the tingling vibration through the soles of his thin plimsols. *UB-44* angled sharply in response to the hydroplanes and he grabbed a steel pillar to maintain his footing. The long red needle of the depth gauge began dropping like the indicator of a high speed lift.

Five feet ten ... fifteen ... twenty . .. Bauer felt the sweat trickling down his crotch as he waited for the shuddering jolt of the exploding bombs and his cotton underpants stuck unpleasantly to his moist flesh. It was the moment every U-boat man hated. The gut-twisting uncertainty that turned their bowels to water in a naked panic of fear.

The men grouped in the control room stared upwards as if the stout steel roof was made of glass and they could see the scene taking place on the surface above. Their faces, grey- white from days imprisoned inside the airless narrow hull, seemed to grow even paler and a thin sheen of sweat glistened on their skins. No one spoke a word. *CRUM-M-M-P! CRUM-M-M-P!*

UB-44. tilted sharply to starboard as the bombs exploded. But the lights stayed on and, apart from the metallic clatter of steel saucepans being thrown to the floor in the galley, the U-boat seemed unharmed. She swung quickly back on to an even keel and Bauer glanced at Hauptmann, the navigator, bracing himself against the chart table.

'They'll have to do better than that,' he grinned with relief. 'I reckon we're safe enough now - although it's lucky they're using surface-fused bombs and not depth-charges.'

Even as he spoke Bauer was aware of something odd. Something missing that he could not put his finger on immediately. Turning round he absorbed every familiar detail of the crowded control room as he tried to pin-point the reason for his sudden feeling of unease.

The inclometer showed *UB-44* holding level trim and

the red needles of depth indicators pointed firmly to the 50 feet calibration mark. All the warning lights on the Diving Control Table were functioning correctly. And the men? Hauptmann was quietly doodling on a blank section of the chart spread out in front of him; Neisser, the Second Coxswain, was at his place in front of the hydroplane controls; *Steuermann* Dichter, squatting behind the wheel, was concentrating on the gyro repeater as he held the U-boat on course. Herzog, standing at the back and leaning on No 4 watertight door, was keeping a watchful eye on things as usual. He was smiling quietly to himself as if enjoying the experience of being under attack.

Bauer checked off the others. Everything was functioning perfectly. And everyone was at their proper stations. Everyone? *That was it.*

'Where is *Kapitanleutnant* Bergman?[5] he asked sharply.

The men looked around the control room and exchanged shrugs. Herzog pushed himself away from the bulkhead. The complacent smile had faded but there was still a glint of satisfaction in his eyes.

'I thought he came down just in front of me, sir.'

'Did anyone else see him?[5] Bauer demanded.

The men shook their heads. With an emergency dive on their hands there had been no time to notice anything except the particular task on which they were engaged. But surely someone would have seen him. And, in any case, it was a matter of routine for Bergman to remain in the control room ready to take over from the Watch Officer as soon as *UB-44* was fully submerged.

Bauer's face was sheet white as he rounded on Herzog. 'You stupid bloody bastard!'

'I'm sure he was in front of me, sir,' Herzog persisted

obstinately. But he was careful to avoid the *leutnant*'s accusing eyes.

'Did *you* clip the upper hatch?'

'Yes, sir. Captain's orders, sir.'

So it hadn't been Bergman's voice echoing down confirmation that the hatch was shut and clipped. Bauer cursed himself for the mistake. But he wasted no time on recriminations with either himself or Herzog. That, he promised grimly, could come later.

'Planes to rise! Periscope depth! Steer five points to starboard.'

'Five points to starboard,' *Steurmann* Dichter intoned.

'Hydroplanes set to rise, sir.'

'Blow No 7, No 9, and No 12 tanks.'

Compressed air hissed through the pipes as the release valves were opened. The three ballast tanks were blown clear of water and, lightened sufficiently, *UB-44* responded to the upward tilt of the hydroplanes. The needles of the depth gauges flickered momentarily and began to climb while Bauer took his place in front of the periscope eye-piece and waited.

He knew that the odds were stacked high against it but, given luck, a man marooned on deck *could* survive if everything went in his favour. But if was a big 'if'. Otto Kretschmer had lived to tell the tale when *U-35* submerged during a training exercise in the Baltic before the war. And, even more remarkably, Baron von Spiegel, a leading ace of the Kaiser War, had been picked up unin-jured when *U-93* sank beneath his feet during a fight with the Q-ship *Prize* in 1917. Perhaps Bergman would be one of the lucky ones.

'Stop blowing... 'planes amidships! Up periscope!'

Neisser centred the big diving wheels and reached up

to shut off the blowing valves. *UB-44* settled obediently at thirty feet and Luttmann pulled the lever controlling the periscope. The column rose smoothly from its well in the floor of the control room Bauer's hands grasped the handles. He took a quick sweep of the horizon and then focused on the flying-boat with the high magnification attack lens. His forehead creased in a puzzled frown. Why the hell had they come down on the sea? Couldn't be engine trouble because all four propellers were spinning. And as *UB-44* had dived without opening fire there was no chance of the Sunderland being damaged.

Bauer ran his eyes along the length of the camouflaged fuselage searching for a clue. He examined the power-driven Nash & Thompson gun turret in the bows - nothing wrong there so far as he could see. Then, turning the periscope slightly, he concentrated on the perspex canopy covering the cockpit — that was sound too. And so were the thickly solid wing roots where the great monoplane wings melded into the fuselage. He shifted his examination further aft. The red white and blue identification roundel just behind the wings gleamed in the bright light and the sun, reflecting off the surface of the sea, left a moving silvery pattern on the drab olive paint like a million fish swimming in the air.

Bauer stopped swinging the periscope when he saw the opened hatch and the two men inside lifting something out. He stepped back clear of the periscope.

'What do you make of this, pilot?' he asked Hauptmann.

The Navigator peered carefully through the eye-piece. 'They seem to be throwing some sort of package out... hang on a minute. I think it's ... yes, it is. It's an inflatable dinghy.'

'Stand away, pilot.' Down periscope.'

No sense in revealing the U-boat's presence if it was not suspected. Although the flying-boat was virtually defenceless while she was drifting on the sea it could still be some sort of trap. Or, and Bauer felt his heart leap at the thought, it could mean ...

'Perhaps they've spotted the skipper, Hermann,' Hauptmann said voicing his companion's unspoken thoughts. 'I reckon they're launching their dinghy to pick him up.'

Bauer took a swift decision,

'Up periscope!'

Pressing his right eye tightly against the lens he searched the empty surface of the sea with the eager concentration of a cat stalking a bird. It was worse than looking for a needle in a haystack but success promised a far greater prize. Suddenly he saw a man's head lift into view as the crest of a wave carried Bergman's body upwards. It vanished into a trough a second later but the brief glimpse had been sufficient.

'I can see him!' he yelled triumphantly. 'I can see the skipper - he's okay.'

The anxious faces of the men in the control room lightened with relief and whispered messages passed fore and aft carrying the news to the rest of the crew. They heard an excited whoop of joy from the off-duty men lying in their bunks in the bow torpedo compartment but the iron discipline of the control room forbid such demonstrations and the release of their pent-up emotions had to be satisfied with tight thin smiles.

Bauer kept his eye glued to the lonely figure in the sea and, as he stared through the lens, he saw the yellow life-raft sweep down and Bergman's hands reach out to grab the line.

'We'll have to work fast,' Hauptmann urged anxiously. 'If we don't get to him first the British will scoop him up as a prisoner.'

They have already, thought Bauer. But he gave no hint of what he had seen through the periscope lens. Hauptmann was right. They had to work fast. He stepped back from the persicope.

'Gun crew close up,' he ordered in a firm tone that masked the anxiety in his heart. 'Blow all tanks! Hydroplanes hard arise.' Unhooking the microphone he held it close to his lips. 'Motor room? Give me maximum power and to hell with draining the batteries. I will probably need to go about when we get on the surface so we'll be staying on the motors.'[2]

Klaus Essen and the crew of the deck gun pushed into the already crowded control room as *UB-44* rose swiftly to the surface. It was the first time the gunner had had an opportunity to demonstrate his skill with the Krupp 105mm quick-firer since the day they had successfully attacked the freighter *Haven Court*[3] with shell-fire. And he was grinning with anticipation.

'I want a couple of machine-guns topsides as well,' Bauer ordered. And two more members of *UB-44's* crew squeezed themselves into the sardine-can space beneath the conning- tower - each grasping a Navy Issue Spandau heavy machine-gun.

The young Executive Officer ran an anxious hand through his short blond hair. It was a terrible responsibility to bear. But no risk was too great if there was even the faintest chance of saving the skipper. Official instructions were terse and to the point. *The safety of the U-boat must never be hazarded for the sake of saving human life.* Well, for once, he was throwing the rule book over the side. And if the Authorities didn't like it they knew what they could do!

Climbing the ladder he reached up to unfasten the dog catches securing the lower hatch. Then, squatting back on the rungs, he used the ladder as a podium to address the men waiting below.

'The enemy seems to be off-guard at the moment but, so far as I could see, the machine-gun turrets are manned. And that means they can open fire instantly. So *UB-44* has got to hit them hard the moment we break surface - *and keep on hitting!* Bauer paused for a moment and looked at the faces staring up at him. He could read the determination in their eyes and he knew he could rely on them. 'You all know the disturbance a U-boat creates as it comes up so we can be quite sure that the enemy will have plenty of warning that we are surfacing. And it's my guess they'll be shooting before we've even managed to get the hatch open,'

The Executive Officer swung the heavy lever of the lower hatch into the 'open' position and placed the palm of his hand against the centre of the steel cover ready to thrust it open.

'Essen - I shall want you with me on the bridge. If your lads go out by the starboard door they'll have some cover from the conning-tower to begin with. But then they'll have to make a dash for it across the open deck. It'll be bloody rough but I want that gun got into action regardless of casualties. Understood?' Essen nodded gravely. Young Bauer was going to make a first-class skipper one of these days. 'I'll see that the machine-guns give you covering fire but there's bound to be a delay while the operators get them mounted. Hauptmann!'

'Sir?'

'Call for volunteers to work the deck gun - we're certain to need a reserve crew. And send one up each time Essen when I give you the shout. I shall want you standing by to take over if anything happens to me. And, no matter what happens, we don't submerge until the skipper is safely back on board. Okay?'

The Navigator nodded and hurried forward into the crew's quarters to round up the volunteers.

'Fifteen feet, sir,' yelled Neisser from the Diving Table.

Bauer glanced at the depth gauge for confirmation. The top of the conning-tower should just be breaking surface. Suddenly he realized the enormity of the decision he had taken in the calm warmth of the control room five minutes earlier. It was easier when someone else was giving the orders. His stomach heaved and he could taste the bile rising sourly into his mouth. Death. That was what it was all about. Funny they never told you about such things at Training School.

His hand jerked up and thrust open the lower hatch. Then, with Essen following closely on his heels, he scrambled up through the darkness of the lower conning- tower compartment and reached up for the final clips.

'Now!'

THREE

The clips of the upper hatch moved smoothly and Bauer threw the steel lid back. Water washed down through the circular opening and drenched the men clinging to the ladder beneath him but he ignored the deluge and hauled himself up on to the bridge - his eyes blinking in the bright sunlight as he crouched behind the bullet-proof screen. Essen followed a moment later. Crawling to the starboard side of the conning-tower he raised his head cautiously and peered over the edge of the screen to check that the door in the base of the "tower at deck level was safely clear of the sea.

UB-44's shark-shaped bows thrust out of the water and then plunged down again as the U-boat levelled on to an even keel. The sea flooded back along the smooth steel foredeck like an incoming tide, lost its momentum, and streamed down the sides of the rounded hull in a bubbling froth. Riding bare inches above the surface the major part of the submarine's hull was still awash but, already, there was just enough clearance to open the vital door.

Essen swung back to the open hatchway, pushed his head down inside, and yelled to the men huddled together in the lower compartment.

'Gun crew - at the double! *Raus!... Raus!'*

Aachan released the locking lever and dragged the door open. Then, leading the other men, he dashed out from behind the cover of the conning-tower, splashed across the slippery deck, and threw himself into position behind the gun...

UB-44 had vomited to the surface in a flurry of erupting spray like a prehistoric sea monster emerging from the depths after centuries of sleep and Murray, the Sunderland's skipper, was the only one to grasp the significance of its unexpected reappearance.

'U-boat surfacing - port side, ten o'clock!'

His urgent warning was met by a stunned silence as the other crew members stared at the enemy submarine with disbelief. Its dramatic appearance from nowhere struck them with the mind-bending shock of a sudden close-up in a horror movie. They froze like marble statues.

'Wake up, you bloody clots!' Murray's voice in their earphones broke the spell. 'Use the machine-guns! And keep them away from that bloody deck gun or we've had it. Toby - cut the line to the dinghy and then stick the spare Vickers out of the hatch. The rest of you, hang on to everything. I'm going to get the hell out of here.'

Flight Sergeant Hallam steered the bow position Nash & Thompson turret on to the port beam arc. The squat, rust- scarred conning-tower centred fair and square in the backsight of his single Browning -303 machine-gun and his thumb felt gently for the button. The U-boat was still outside the arc of fire of the rear turret with its clutch of quadruple machine-guns but Ned Kelley, the Aussie 'tail-end Charlie', swung it tight up against the safety stop and hunched over his guns waiting. Maitland, in the waist hatch, had a clear field of fire. Slotting the manually operated Vicker's K-gun quickly into position he hosed a line of tracer bullets towards UB-44.

Essen ducked the instant Maitland opened fire and he heard the angry thud of bullets against the plating of the conning-tower. Behind him, Lutz whipped up the Spandau, rested the barrel on the lip of the screen, and returned fire. The enemy hesitated for a moment - then answered with redoubled fury as Hallam brought the nose turret into action.

Keeping well down behind the protection of the conning- tower screen Bauer crawled across to the voice-pipes.

'Obey bridge.' He slid the cover of the observation slit to one side and peered out. The yellow dinghy, its umbilical cord to the flying-boat cut, was drifting downwind towards the stern and he could see Bergman crouched low inside it as the bullets whistled over his head, trapping him in the crossfire. 'Steer two points to port. And stay on full power.'

Lutz's machine-gun drilled a neat line of holes into the Alclad skin of the Sunderland's fuselage just below the cockpit as UB~44 swung her bows towards her winged opponent and, almost simultaneously, the four engines of the flying- boat thundered to life. Clouds of white exhaust smoke streamed astern and, unsighted by the smoke screen, Maitland stopped firing while he waited for the exhaust to clear.

Obergefreiter Hugo Aachan, No I layer of the 105mm quick-firer, the first man to reach the gun, threw himself into the seat and swung the weapon towards the aircraft.

But, isolated in the bow turret of the flying-boat Hallam's view was unobstructed by the engine smoke and the -303 Browning juddered frantically as his thumb pressed the firing button again. And, at the precise moment the rest of the U- boat's gun team emerged into the open to join Aachan, a hail of bullets raked the deck forward of the conning-tower.

Erich Mucken, the loader, screamed as two heavy bullets tore into his stomach. He jerked sideways under the impact, lost his footing on the slippery deck plates, flailed his arms wildly in the air to maintain balance, and slid over the side into the tumbling white waters that streamed past the fast moving U-boat. Sven Koeller also went down in the same murderous burst of fire with a bullet-shattered shoulder but, biting back the pain, he crawled forward along the deck and hauled himself into position at Aachan's side.

Willi Schmidt, waiting in the control room as the first volunteer, shivered as he heard the thud and whine of bullets on deck. He thought of Gerda and wondered how she was getting on. Perhaps he was a father already - you could never tell with babies.

Essen's head thrust down through the upper hatch. 'First two reserves on deck!'

Hauptmann banged Willi on the shoulder and the young seaman scrambled up through the hatch, plunged out of the open conning-tower door, and raced for the gun as if all the devils in hell were at his heels.

Flight Sergeant Hallam had the bit firmly between his teeth. Letting out a whoop of excitement as he dropped, first, Mucken, and then Koeller, he drew a fresh bead on the next man to appear from behind the shield of the conning- tower. It was like shooting little white ducks in a fairground rifle range. He depressed his thumb again.

Essen's face reflected no emotion as he saw Schmidt go down. Shouting for another reserve he turned to watch the flying-boat gathering speed ready for take-off. And the thought that the quarry might escape decided him.

'I'm going down to give a hand with the gun, sir.'

Bauer was too busy steering the submarine to consider the wisdom of Essen's action. He nodded briefly and returned to his task of bringing *UB-44* closer to the enemy.

Placing one hand on the overhanging lip of the conning- tower screen Essen vaulted to the deck and raced to Aachan's assistance. Kurt Momsen, miraculously unscathed by the raking burst of fire that had cut down Schmidt, was already at the gun and he jerked up the breech lever as Essen broke open the lid of the ready-use ammunition. The box contained three types of ammunition — the distinctive red banded high explosive shell for general use, the yellow nosed AP-15 designed to pierce enemy armour, and the green ringed proximity fused Type 4-Z for anti-aircraft fire.

The Petty Officer grabbed one of the high explosive marks and tossed it to Momsen. It was heavy and cumbersome. But Momsen, a Bremen stevedore in civilian life, caught it deftly, swung his body from the hips, and thrust it into the gaping mouth of the breech. Slamming the block into place he pulled down the locking lever.

'Okay, Hugo. It's up the spout.'

It was an unorthodox way in which to report the gun loaded and ready. But this was no time for the niceties of the drill book. Everyone knew what he meant. The range was point-blank - about 100 yards - and Aachan disdained to use the telescopic sight. He had already lined the gun up while Momsen was loading and, in response to the shout, he closed his hand over the firing lever.

Staring down the barrel of the Browning machine-gun Flight Sergeant Hallam drew a careful bead on the group of men desperately working the U-boat's gun. His thumb depressed the button. The Nash & Thompson turret vibrated with noise and the stink of burnt cordite irritated his nose but he kept his thumb down firmly as *UB-44*'s gun fired its first shot. He saw one of the three men spin to the deck as the bullets found their mark and he grinned. It was the last conscious thing he did.

The U-boat's shell smashed into the squat nose of the flying boat and exploded with the clatter of a thousand tin cans being kicked down a narrow alley. Flames erupted in every direction and the heavy power-driven turret was torn from its seating and hurled high into the air. It fell back to the sea with an ugly splash and sank to the bottom like a stone.

The force of the explosion shattered the canopy of the cockpit and Murray, the blood dripping from his face where splinters of perspex had slashed his forehead, pushed the throttles wide open in a last desperate attempt to get the Sunderland into the air. But it was a futile effort. A wall of flame rose in front of his eyes and, ripping off the safety harness, he hauled himself up out of the pilot's seat to escape the advancing holocaust.

Crouched low behind the bullet-proof screen of the conning-tower Lutz nestled the butt of the Spandau deeper into his shoulder and fired blindly into the flames. A line of bullets sprayed the cockpit and Murray slumped forward across the instrument panel with blood welling from his chest. Despite his wounds, and realizing that the accelerating speed of the flying-boat was fanning the flames aft, the pilot made a last heroic attempt to save his aircraft by pulling back the throttle levers. The Sunderland's mad rush across the water suddenly slowed and she swung in a wild curve towards her enemy as the melted control wires allowed the rudder to flap free.

Essen, his face masked with blood where Hallam's bullet had creased his scalp, picked himself up from the deck, lifted another shell from the ready-use box, and passed it to Momsen with unhurried ease as if the bloody chaos surrounding the gun did not exist.

Mucken's body had long since floated astern. Koeller, bent double with the agony of his wounded shoulder, had given up his attempt to help with the gun and, burying his head into the crook of his unwounded arm, he crouched on the deck crying with pain. Willi Schmidt, lying face down in a pool of blood, was dead.

Aachan's arms moved like pistons as he spun the traversing wheel of the 105mm and the long grey barrel swung rapidly to right and left as he tried to hold the demented wanderings of the flying-boat in his sights. He steadied the gun long enough for Momsen to slide the second shell into the breech and, as the locking lever was secured, he swung back in pursuit of his winged quarry.

'Ready!'

Sighting straight down the barrel Aachan aimed at the gleaming red, white and blue roundel painted on the slabsided fuselage. It was impossible to miss even from the pitching, rolling gun platform of the U-boat's deck.

Crack! The shell took the flying-boat full in her belly and the explosion ripped the hull in half. The forward section tipped over under the weight of engines and disappeared beneath the surface in a matter of seconds.

The aft portion, dominated by the tall single fin of the rudder, tilted drunkenly as the sea rushed into the fuselage but remained defiantly afloat and Essen could see the rear-gunner frantically fighting to free the jammed escape hatch of his turret. Poor bastard, he thought to himself.

Bauer, too, was watching from the bridge. And satisfied that the enemy could do *UB-44.* no more harm, he rapped out a series of orders that swung the U-boat in a tight circle and brought the dinghy into a suitable position for recovery on the lee side. Once Bergman was safely on board there would be time to try to save the men still alive in the remains of the flying-boat.

'Stop motors. Switches off - clutches in. Half ahead both. Steer 8 points to port.'

'Half ahead both. Steer Port-8.'

UB-44's bows moved through an arc of ninety degrees in response to the rudder as the high pitched whine of the motors faded away. The diesel units coughed to life. A jet of black oil smoke spat from the exhausts but was quickly replaced by a shimmering blue haze of hot gases as the finely tuned MAN engines settled into their throbbing stride. The U-boat moved ahead, picking up speed as the propellers bit into the water, and a faint wash frothed at the bows like a white moustache. Leaning over the edge of the conning- tower screen, Bauer surveyed the shambles on deck.

Torn metal marked the path of the enemy's machine-gun bullets and he counted over thirty deeply gouged holes in the plating that bridged the distance from the conning-tower door to the gun. And they were only the ones that had hit the submarine.

'Helm amidships.' Bauer corrected the course as *UB-*

44's bows lined up on the rubber dinghy in the middle distance.

The Executive Officer shivered as he stared down at the scarred plating. If they'd been hit thirty times, how many more bullets had sliced across the U-boat's deck at body height? It was a miracle that anyone had survived at all. Willi Schmidt's body still lay motionless under the-shadow of the Krupp quick-firer he had volunteered to serve and Bauer thought of the baby in Hamburg that would never see its father.

Aachan bent across the sprawled body, searching for life and Essen, wiping the blood from his face, joined him.

'No use, Chief,' the gunlayer said simply. 'He's gone.'

UB-44's gunner knelt in silence beside the body. He said nothing but his eyes were wet with unspoken grief. Only that morning, enjoying the warmth of the sun on deck, he had promised Willi that he would act as god-father when the baby was baptized at the old Lutheran church in the Drummer Platz. The ceremony had been arranged for their next spell of shore leave; with the sweet smell of victory in the air, Willi had already taken bets that this would be *UB-44*'s last combat patrol. And now he would be there alone, standing alongside the mourning widow, swearing his solemn promises for a fatherless child. Of all people - why did it have to be Willi?

'Essen!'

The Petty Officer looked up in response to Bauer's shout from the bridge. 'Sir?'

'Is he dead?'

'Yes, sir.'

Bauer lowered his voice. It seemed somehow irreverent to shout.

'Put the body over the side, Chief. You know our Standing Orders.'

Essen understood. There was no need to explain. A submarine had no room for sentiment. And the cramped and crowded compartments were no place to store a corpse to await decent burial. It was hard. But that was the way it had to be.

Aachan tied two iron bars to Schmidt's legs while Essen grasped the shoulders. Then, without speaking a word, they carried their dead comrade gently to the edge of the deck and stood, balanced uneasily, each with one foot on the slippery curve of the ballast tanks. Rising above the primitive brutality of the scene they instilled a certain simple dignity into the task of sliding Willi's body to its last resting place beneath the sea. And despite the pagan symbolism of the black swastika under which they sailed, Aachan crossed himself while Essen mumbled a quick half-remembered prayer from the service for burials at sea. As he watched the dark weighted shape sink silently beneath the surface the gunner suddenly recalled the words of an old poem:

No hero's death for those who die
  In service for their flag.
  No wreaths, no flags, no bugle calls,
  Just peace beneath the sea.

Then, their grim task completed, the two men climbed back on to the deck and, with Momsen's help, they carried the wounded Koeller carefully back to the lower conning- tower compartment where *Sanitatsober-*

maat Steiner was waiting with his surgical kit spread out neatly on the steel- plated floor.

'Stop engines.'

UB-44 slowed and Bauer watched the rubber dinghy run in under the protective lee of the U-boat's port side.

'Foredeck party! Stand by to recover dinghy.'

The seamen waiting in the lower conning-tower compartment where Steiner had set up his temporary casualty clearing station, made their way to the starboard door. The deck was slippery with blood and the air reeked with the acrid bite of antiseptics. But ignoring the shuffling of their feet as they hurried past, Steiner concentrated on Koeller's shoulder, probing the shattered bone for the bullet, while Aachan held a cotton wool pad soaked in ether over the man's mouth.

Essen pulled the door open. 'Get a move on, lads. And go easy on the skipper - he's had a rough time.'

Bedraggled and exhausted, *Kapitanleutnant* Bergman crouched in the bottom of the dinghy retched up the sea water that clogged his lungs. His hands were cut and bleeding and his ribs still ached from the concussion of the bomb blast that had saved his life. With an effort of will-power he dragged himself upright as the foredeck party prepared to receive him.

Holding the rubber life-raft against the side of the U-boat's hull with a boat-hook Schomberg grinned widely as Bergman looked up. 'Throw down a line!'

Although his voice was hoarse it still contained the sharp quality of command and a rope snaked down obediently.

Bergman grasped it firmly. He could have secured it to one of the wooden mooring cleats but he was determined, whatever it might cost, to come aboard unaided and set the men an example. It was an act of mock heroics and he knew it. But years of training as a career officer made the gesture imperative.

'Haul away.'

Kornfeldt and the other seamen leaned back to take the strain as Bergman's bare feet slithered on the weed-covered surface of the ballast tanks. And for one heady moment the *Kapitanleutnant* felt himself back in the Bavarian mountains climbing the north face of the Gunnenberg. Then strong hands clasped his waist and he was back on *UB-44*'s friendly deck.

'Welcome aboard, sir.'

Bergman liked the understatement in Schomberg's greeting. He would have liked to respond in a similar vein. But the emotion of finding himself back on board his own ship was too great to permit words. And above all he had to preserve his image. His voice, still hoarse from the salt, was brusque.

'Thank you, Schomberg. You can let go the dinghy. The rest of you get below at the double.'

Turning away, he limped down the deck towards the conning-tower, paused for a moment to look at the bullet-torn plating, and ducked through the open door. Essen saluted smartly as the skipper entered the lower compartment and Bergman acknowledged him gravely.

'Excellent shooting, Chief. I had a grandstand view of what happened.'

'Thank you, sir.'

Steiner looked up from the pulped mess of Koeller's shoulder as he laid a sterile dressing on the gaping wound. 'I'd better check you over, sir.'

Bergman shook his head. 'Later, Steiner, later. I've

only had a ducking. You'd best get your patient below before we submerge.'

'I don't think we should move him, sir. He's an amputation case. I've stopped the bleeding for the moment but if it starts up again I don't give much for his chances.'

'Get him below, Steiner. That's an order!'

Bergman grabbed the conning-tower ladder and hauled himself up on to the bridge. It wasn't healthy to remain on the surface any longer and the sooner UB-44 took to the depths again the better. But why was he always being faced by the same agonized choice? He'd nearly lost his boat, not to mention his life, by hesitating to search for the missing Raulheim. And yet, on a previous occasion, his disregard for human life when he abandoned Werth had saved the U-boat from instant destruction. It didn't matter a damn what the preachers might say - it was no use having a conscience when the lives of forty men rested in your hands. And from now on there could be only one decision when the chips were down. The safety of the boat was all that counted. Perhaps only God had the right to grant life or death. But on UB-44 even God had to obey the captain's orders!

'Bauer!'

The Executive Officer turned and his face broke into a grin of genuine relief as he saw Bergman heave himself up through the hatch.

He put his mouth to the voice-tube. 'Half ahead both. Steer five points to starboard.'

Then, having given his orders, he bent to help Bergman up out of the hatch opening.

'Good to see you, sir. I thought...'

"Why have you changed course?' Bergman demanded, cutting him short in mid-sentence.

'The after section of the flying-boat is still afloat, sir. The rear-gunner seems to be trapped. I was going to try and go alongside to get him out.'

Bergman looked around the bridge. 'How long have we been surfaced?' he asked.

'About an hour I suppose, sir.'

'And where are the lookouts?'

Bauer hesitated. In his excitement to get to the surface and rescue the skipper he had forgotten about lookouts.

Bergman pushed him aside and bent over the voice-pipe.

'This is the captain. Stop engines and stand by for diving. All hands to diving stations.' He turned to Lutz and the other machine-gunner who were leaning their backs against the bridge screen checking their weapons. 'You two! Take over sky watch duties. And look sharp.'

'But what about the man in the rear turret, sir?' Bauer asked.

'To hell with the man in the turret,' Bergman snapped. 'I will not have my boat put in hazard a second longer. Given the right conditions I would do my best to save him. But the boat is damaged and we have two wounded men. We submerge!'

You rotten bastard, thought Bauer. He stared across at the remains of the flying-boat sticking forlornly out of the water. It was sinking lower every minute and the sea had reached up to lap the chest of the trapped man. Every instinct urged him to countermand Bergman's callous order but now that the skipper was back on board, he no longer had the ultimate power of decision. The iron restraints of discipline imprisoned his natural emotions as effectively as the jammed escape hatch was trapping Kelly inside his perspex coffin. He saluted, pushed his feet obediently into the gaping maw of the upper hatch, and slid down the ladder to the control room.

'Clear the bridge!'

Lutz and his fellow lookout left their positions and followed the Executive Officer below leaving Bergman standing alone on the deserted bridge. The Sunderland's stern turret was barely showing above the surface now and he knew that the air-gunner had already drowned. So they would have been too late anyway. It was small consolation for a barbarous decision but Bergman knew his choice had been correct. Perhaps he had been morally wrong. But, for a U-boat captain, morals had to take second place to the safety requirements of his command - just as conscience sometimes had to bow before the demands of patriotism. He had murdered in the name of Germany. And he had sacrificed men in cold blood for the sake of the majority. What further crimes, he wondered, would he be called upon to commit before this anguish was over?

Securing the upper hatch he dropped into the control room and reached up to clip the lower cover. *UB-44* was already down to periscope depth and he adjusted to the familiar routine as if his ordeal of the previous two hours had never happened.

'Any leaks from the damaged plates?'

'No, sir. The pressure hull seems undamaged. But we're still having trouble with those two starboard pumps.'

Bergman nodded. 'Take over the Watch, Number One, while I go and put on some dry clothes. Better run a full damage check and let me have a report. I'd rather be safe than sorry.'

Squeezing down the narrow passage past the radio

office he met Steiner on his way to the control room. The *Sanitatsobermaat* looked tired and he was wiping fresh blood from his arm where it had splashed over the top of his rubber gloves. Bergman stopped.

'How is Koeller?' he asked quietly.

Steiner shook his head. 'The bleeding has started again, sir. There's not very much chance.'

Bergman clasped his arm tightly. 'Do your best for him,' he urged. 'We should be back at Wilhelmshaven in three days. If you can keep him alive until then he'll have a good chance. They can perform miracles at the Base Hospital.

Stepping into the wardroom Bergman pulled the curtain shut and quickly stripped off his wet clothing. He rummaged in his locker for a fresh outfit. The cool draught of the fan goose-pimpled his skin and he shivered. Suddenly his entire body surrendered in nervous reaction to his ordeal and he began to shake uncontrollably. His legs almost gave way and his teeth chattered. But determined not to give in to his weakness, he reached for a bottle of Schnapps standing on the table, pulled off the cork, and swallowed the spirit in mouthfuls. It burned his stomach but the comforting glow that followed quickly steadied his nerves and the shivering stopped.

Shaken by the violence of his reaction Bergman sat down for a few moments to allow the liquor to complete its work. Then, finding a towel, he dried himself vigorously to restore his circulation, slipped on a fresh pair of trousers and a warmly dry sweater, and made his way back to the control room. He was grateful that the privacy of the wardroom had masked his unexpected and uncharacteristic attack of nerves from the eyes of the crew.

UB-44 was running at 4 knots and trimmed level at

thirty feet. Bauer was carrying out a routine periscope check and he completed quartering the horizon before ordering it to be lowered and joining the skipper at the chart table where he was discussing their position with the U-boat's navigator.

'The pilot reckons we're just about here,' Bergman explained, stabbing the sharp tip of the dividers into the chart at a point some 100 miles from Land's End. 'We're too short on fuel to run north-about Scotland so I'll have to risk going up through the Straits. It's my guess that the British will be too busy preparing their anti-invasion defences to worry about hunting for U-boats on their doorstep. Any comments?'

Bauer knew why the skipper was gambling on a quick run home via the Dover Straits. He had overheard the conversation with Steiner. And he wanted to know why Bergman was proposing to hazard the boat for the sake of one man. But he never got the opportunity to ask the pertinent question. Meister, *UB-44*'s senior radio operator, hurried into the control room and thrust a slip of paper in Bergman's hands. 'Signal from *BdU* sir. Just come in. I've decoded it.' Bergman took the pink flimsy and read it. He passed it across to Bauer without comment.

76-50-79-7-40   *From BdU to Commanding Officer UB-44*

Immediate. Return to Lorient on completion of patrol. Signal rendezvous time at Belle Ile. Minesweeper will meet and escort you into base. Recognition signal and rendezvous position to follow.

Doenitz V/A

So this time they were returning to France and not to Germany. To Bergman's perceptive mind the unexpected change in routine confirmed his fears that the war was going to continue no matter what the propaganda broadcasts might say. If the German Admiralty were taking the trouble to equip the French Atlantic dockyards as bases for their U-boats, it could mean only one thing - the British intended to carry on the fight and Doenitz wanted to increase the range of his sea wolves by bringing them closer to the vital mid-Atlantic operational areas. Hitler was clearly anticipating a long war.

'Fancy the conquering hero bit, sir?' Bauer asked forgetting his recent antagonism in the excitement.

Bergman frowned. 'I don't follow, Number One.'

'Well, sir, you know what I mean. Setting up new bases in a defeated country adds a bit of zest to things, doesn't it?' Bergman turned away to avoid answering the question. If this was the attitude of the average German officer then heaven help us, he thought. No wonder half the world hated Germany.

'Give me a course, pilot,' he said handing the decoded signal to Hauptmann. 'I want to be at the rendezvous two hours before high water - we'll need plenty of depth for diving if we come under attack. How soon can we make it?'

'I'll have to check the tide tables, sir, but I'd say, off the cuff, just before noon tomorrow - sooner if we run on the surface in daylight.'

Bergman shook his head. 'Too risky. We stay down until sunset. Once the RAF finds out that the U-boats are using the French Atlantic ports they'll fly standing patrols over the approach routes. And you can bet your life Goering's bloody Luftwaffe won't give us any air support.'

Hauptmann pulled down the heavy volume of tide tables - ironically a British Admiralty issue - and began his calculations.

The news that *UB-44 was* returning to a French port quickly spread to the crew and excited groups gathered to discuss the latest turn of events. Brunner, the wardroom steward and the U-boat's self-appointed stud, greeted the news with a bellowing roar of delight. And then, as the full import of what it meant permeated his brain, he sat down heavily on one of the lower bunks.

'Jesus wept,' he said slowly.

'What's the matter, Max?' someone chided. 'Forgotten how to do it?'

'Have I hell!' he grinned. 'Hey, Karl,' he called to Lutz who was sitting at the mess tables cleaning his machine-gun. 'You're the guy who went to High School — ain't it right that it's legal in France?'

'You mean *les maisons de tolerance?* Sure, they're legal. You don't mean to say you're going to *pay* for it.'

Brunner suddenly saw what Lutz meant. He let out a vast belly laugh and slapped a ham-sized hand against his thigh. 'Like hell I am - always got it for free at home. Just think of it. All those French skirts lining up and waiting for it.' He laughed again. 'You know, it was worth winning the war.' Lutz slipped the recoil spring into the breech of the Spandau and locked the sliding bolt into position. Putting the gun down on the scrubbed table top he picked up a small cotton bag in which he normally carried his plimsolls. He held it towards Brunner.

'Well, before you start throwing your money at some fancy French piece, I'll have your contribution.'

Max stared at the bag dangling in front of him. 'What for?'

'For Willi's kid - that's what for.'

Brunner looked suitably chastened. *'Ja,* for Willi's kid,' he nodded soberly. Digging deep into his pocket he pulled out a thick roll of *Reichsmarks* and threw the notes down on the table. 'Here, Karl. Take the lot. I reckon his wife will need it more than me. Why it had to be Willi and not some useless bum like me I'll never know.'

The others added their contributions to the pile of money lying on the table. Willi Schmidt had been a popular shipmate and not one of them begrudged donating towards the kitty. The usually rowdy compartment was suddenly silent with unspoken memories.

It was Brunner who finally broke the silence. He slapped his thigh and laughed. 'Well, I guess that settles it, lads. Now I'll *have* to get it for free!'

Bergman was checking Hauptmann's projected course on the charts as *Sanitatsobermaat* Steiner entered the control room.

'Yes, Steiner?'

'It's Koeller, sir. He's dead. I couldn't stop the bleeding, sir.'

Bergman straightened up. 'You did all you could, Steiner. Don't blame yourself - it was my fault for disregarding your advice about shifting him.'

'We're due to surface in about three hours, sir,' Bauer pointed out. 'We can put the body over the side as soon as it's dark.'

'No need for that, Number One. We should be in Lorient tomorrow. I would prefer him to receive a proper naval funeral.'

'But you know Standing Orders, sir,' Bauer protested.

'Bodies must not be kept on board an operational U-boat. Paragraph 3 - "a deceased man should be buried at sea at the first opportunity".'

Few people had ever seen Bergman lose his temper before and the men in the control room flinched as his eyes blazed in sudden anger.

'Don't dare to question my instructions, *Leutnant* Bauer! This is my boat and Koeller is one of *my* men. To hell with Standing Orders - I will not see one of my crew consigned to the sea simply because some faceless bureaucrat in Berlin decides that it is bad for morale to have a corpse on board a U-boat. *I* say he will be buried properly on shore.'

The Executive Officer kept his mouth shut. The skipper seemed to obey or disobey orders at will. Or was there some deeper motive behind his apparently willful actions. A thousand questions ran through Bauer's mind. Bergman had never been the same since that odd affair in the Gulf of Mexico and yet there seemed no logical reason why he should have been so affected by the loss of the *Koenig*. After all, he reminded himself, *UB-44* hadn't sunk the pocket- battleship - she'd scuttled herself. One thing, however, was beyond question. *Kapitanleutnant* Bergman was becoming a very difficult man to serve under.

'Bow torpedo room?'

Pederson's disembodied voice acknowledged through the loudspeaker system. 'Bow torpedo room, sir.'

'Are all tubes kitted up?'

'Yes, sir. We reloaded the last of the spares this morning after the attack on the tanker.'

Bergman thought for a moment. 'I want you to draw the torpedo from Starboard Two,' he instructed. 'And keep the tube pumped dry.' He turned to Steiner. 'I propose to keep Koeller's body in the empty torpedo tube until we get into Lorient. It will be quite safe and out of the way and,' he shot a meaningful glance at Bauer, 'it should not offend anyone's sensibilities. Have you got anything to cover him with?'

'Yes, sir. There are some canvas shrouds in the medical stores. I'll get one prepared.'

Bergman nodded. 'Good. And tell Essen to bring up a spare ensign. I'll leave you to carry out the details and I'm sure you'll be able to get his messmates to help.' He turned to Bauer. 'I want you to go up forward and supervise. And find some volunteers to act as guard of honour.'

The expression on Bauer's face mirrored his resentment and as he was about to leave the control room to carry out his instructions, Bergman called him back. He spoke quietly so that they could not be overheard.

'You don't seem happy about my decision, *Herr Leutnant!*'

Bauer decided to brave the skipper's wrath. 'It's contrary to orders, sir, that's all.'

Bergman looked at the young officer and rubbed his chin reflectively. He could remember his own resentment when, as a junior watch officer, he had seen Stohr, the skipper of *UB-16,* listening into an enemy radio broadcast.

'I agree, Number One,' he said slowly. 'It *is* against orders. But I am not the only officer on board *UB-44* who disobeys official instructions. I seem to remember a very specific order that the captain of a U-boat must not hazard his boat in order to rescue survivors and that he must always be ready to sacrifice a member of his crew if the safety of the U-boat is at stake. Why, in direct disobedience of that order, did you surface to rescue me this morning?'

'But that was different, sir. You are the captain.'

Bergman smiled and shook his head. 'Correction, *Herr Leutnant*. As soon as I was lost you became the captain. And, as captain, you chose to ignore what is probably the most difficult rule in the book to obey. I'm not reprimanding you - in fact, I should thank you for saving my life. But next time you blow your top bear in mind that, when it comes to the crunch, we all break the rules. At that moment you were the *de facto* commander of *UB-44* and, in contravention of official instructions, you hazarded your boat to save a shipmate.'

He paused for a moment and then continued. 'That is something I would never do. Not because I blindly obey every order I receive but because I, personally, place the safety of my boat above all other considerations. In the case of Koeller no one is being placed in danger and I am not risking the safety of my boat. But Koeller was a shipmate. And in my view I owe him the respect and honour of a decent funeral. So remember - rules are for the guidance of wise men and the obedience of fools. *Orders* are to be obeyed regardless of consequence.'

Bauer's resentment had slowly evaporated as he listened to Bergman's words. But the expression on his face showed that he was still puzzled.

'But, sir, these were both orders. Why obey one and not the other?'

Bergman was silent for a few moments, lost in his thoughts. Once again, in his memory, he heard the thunderclap explosion as *Koenig's* magazines ignited.

'Orders,' he said picking his words carefully, 'must always be obeyed if they are issued in good faith, for the protection of the Fatherland. One's personal opinion of such orders, or the results that flow from them, are of no consequence. They must be obeyed. But any order of purely bureaucratic origin which can be disobeyed without hurt or consequence to Germany becomes a matter of personal choice. Taking our two examples: the risk of sacrificing a U-boat to save a shipmate could weaken the armed strength of the Fatherland and the order which forbids hazarding your ship in such circumstances must therefore be obeyed without question. But the order that says all bodies must be disposed of has no effect on the destiny of Germany. It is just bureaucratic mumbo- jumbo and, worse, it reduces respect for the dignity of the human being. Such an order, in my view, falls within the discretion of my own conscience.'

Bauer nodded dutifully although, secretly, he had strong reservations about the validity of the skipper's arguments. Bergman seemed to have a strange capacity for twisting the meaning of words to suit his purposes - but perhaps it was only an outward symptom of the perverted patriotism that seemed to be the skipper's only moral yardstick. And while Bauer knew that he would always personally do his utmost to obey every lawful order he was given, there must come a time when, for reasons of conscience, it would be impossible to do so. But until that moment came he did not intend to worry about it. That, he supposed, was where the captain scored. He seemed to have no conscience to contend with. In Bergman's eyes only one thing mattered. His love for his country, his Fatherland, Germany.

'Just one more thing, Number One.'

'Sir?'

Bergman smiled suddenly. 'This is the first chance

I've had for congratulating you on the way you handled *UB-44* in my absence. When I give my report to the Flotilla Commander tomorrow I shall be making a personal recommendation that your name is put forward to *BdU* for immediate promotion - and appointment in command of your own U- boat.'

FOUR

Kapitan z.s. Erwin Walther, Commanding Officer of the 10th Flotilla, brought the tips of his fingers together judicially as Bergman concluded his report of *UB-44!*s sixth patrol.

'But surely you are not accusing Herzog of trying to kill you, *Kapitanleutnant.* I have known the man for years and he is probably the best warrant officer in the entire U-boat service. Could there not have been a genuine mistake - a misunderstanding?'

'In my opinion, no, sir,' Bergman said firmly. 'Herzog knew I was on the bridge and by reporting Raulheim as missing he ensured that I would make a further search. He deliberately closed the hatch and left me marooned on deck in the full knowledge that *UB-44* was diving.'

'Did he specifically tell Bauer you were safely below when he reported the hatch clips secured?'

"Not specifically, sir. It was, however, implied.'

Walther, a veteran U-boat officer with a distinguished combat record in the Kaiser war when he had served with the Cattaro Flotilla alongside Doenitz, continued his probing cross-examination. Bergman's account seemed utterly incredible.

'You have, of course, obtained Herzog's explanation, *Kapitanleutnant?*'

'Yes, *Herr Kapitan.* He stuck rigidly to his story that, in the heat of the emergency, he thought I had already gone below. He admits that he now realizes he was wrong. But he cannot, or will not, add anything to his statement.'

Walther took a small black cheroot from the silver box on his desk, struck a match, and applied the flame. He was clearly weighing his words carefully before he spoke again.

'Very well, Bergman. Let us, just for one moment, assume that your accusation is correct. What could possibly be Herzog's motive?'

Bergman hesitated. It was a question he had asked himself over and over again. He felt sure that Herzog somehow knew the truth about the *Koenig* incident but suddenly, as he considered Walther's question, he realized the impossibility of voicing his suspicions. Only one member of *Bd*U's Staff, *Kommodore* Neurath, had been aware of Hitler's signal to *UB-* 44 - and he had been killed in a road accident in Southern Norway two months previously. Walther, although his flotilla commander knew nothing of the secret attack and, so far as he could ascertain, neither did Vice Admiral Doenitz nor any member of his Staff. Bergman swallowed hard. The only persons who knew the details of the secret order were the Fuehrer himself and his immediate naval advisers. And his common-sense warned him that there would be a complete denial of responsibility from that quarter if he dared to reveal that *UB-44*'s torpedoes had sunk the pocket- battleship. The fact that he had been acting in obedience to a direct order from the Fuehrer would never be believed even though he had kept a copy of the fatal signal as evidence.

Whatever might happen, this was not the time either to tell the truth or produce the evidence that he had been acting under orders. Hitler, having conquered half Europe, was at the peak of his triumph and, for the moment, he was invulnerable. One day perhaps, when the sands of time were running out and the Nazi dictator's position was less secure, Bergman's copy of the fatal signal might be one of the weapons that could dislodge Hitler from his leadership of Germany. But in July 1940 with France defeated and Britain on the brink of collapse, Hitler's invincible position could never be undermined by an insignificant U-boat commander who had, in obedience to orders, murdered a thousand innocent German sailors. And Bergman was under no illusion, either, that his own admission of guilt in the *Koenig* affair would be tantamount to signing his own death warrant.

'I'm afraid I can suggest no motive, *Herr Kapitan*' he replied after a long pause.

Walther's eyebrows lifted in surprise but he made no comment.

'Very well, Bergman, we will leave that point aside. Now tell me this. In view of the serious nature of your report why did you not put Herzog under immediate arrest? I seem to recall that you had no hesitation in arresting your previous coxswain, Mittleburger, after the Wilhelmshaven air raid and *he* had certainly not threatened your life'

There was no answer to Walther's shrewdly aimed question and Bergman had sense enough not to try to invent one. But by dredging up the Mittleburger episode the Flotilla Commander was subtly suggesting that his relations with his subordinates were not all they could be. He stared at the floor silently and waited.

'And why did you not make out a court martial charge for my approval?'[5] Walther continued as he exploited the weakness.

Bergman felt he must say something if only to defend his own untenable position. 'Herzog is a good warrant officer in every way, sir. Despite the serious nature of my report, I considered that this matter was entirely personal to myself and in no way affected his loyalty or efficiency.

As the words left his lips Bergman realized he had shot his own case to pieces. In fact he would be lucky to retain command of an operational U-boat at all after the fiasco.

It was fortunate that Walther, as an ex-U-boat captain, had sufficient experience to discern the symptoms of strain in Bergman's face and to understand the stresses involved in the unending struggle of underwater warfare. He looked up and smiled sympathetically.

'If you ask me, Bergman, this whole episode has blown up out of all proportion. I'd say it was nothing more serious than a touch of the *Blechkoller*[1]. A week's leave will clear this rubbish out of your mind. I see you've completed six combat patrols so it's hardly surprising that you're getting jumpy. Happens to the best of us I can assure you.'

'Perhaps you're right, sir,' Bergman lied. It was useless to disagree. He knew that the coxswain had tried to kill him. But proof was another matter. However he still had one card up his sleeve and he played it as casually as he could. 'As you say, sir, we've probably been getting on each other's nerves recently. He's a good warrant officer really. May I suggest that he is transferred to another boat where his experience would be more valuable. After all, sir, my crew are all seasoned veterans now.'

Walther shook his head. 'Your crew *were* veterans, Bergman.' He handed him a sheet of paper bearing the *BdU* crest and signed by Doenitz himself. 'I was going to show you this later, but in the circumstances, I think you should see it now. Both your *Wachoffiziers* will be leaving *UB-44*. Bauer has been promoted to *Oberleutnant* and is getting his own command with the 6th Flotilla. And Hauptmann has been posted for instructional duties at the Navigation School at Bremen. I was pleased to see your recommendation about Bauer in the report but, of course, this promotion and posting was decided several weeks ago. And apart from your two officers, roughly half of *UB-44*'s crew have been transferred to other boats in the flotilla.'

Bergman was glad for Bauer. He was a top rate officer who fully merited a command posting. But to take half his crew as well - what the hell did they think they were doing?

'So Herzog cannot be spared,' Walther explained. 'He will be one of the only experienced senior men left on *UB-44* and you'll need him to help lick the new crew into shape.'

'But why now, sir? If we step up the U-boat offensive we're going to need the very best we've got - crews as well as boats.'

'Precisely, Bergman. New boats are arriving from Germany every day but they all have greenhorn crews and inexperienced officers. If we want to create a striking force that can meet and defeat the Royal Navy, we must give them a chance to learn their jobs under combat conditions. And that means putting some experienced men in the new boats and giving you old hands some new blood for training.' He smiled suddenly. 'Don't worry; you're not the only one to suffer. Kretschmer sails tomorrow with twenty trainees on board *U-99* and Prien's boat has had a crew change as well. It's the only way.'

'I suppose so,' Bergman admitted reluctantly. He had brought his crew to a fine pitch of efficiency and hated to see them go. But if the war was continuing, it was essential to get back into battle without delay. 'How soon will *UB-44* be ready, sir?'

The Flotilla commander picked up the maintenance report and glanced down the schedules. 'Hm ... a couple of bilge pumps to be stripped down and overhauled ... usual electrical replacements. And she'll need scraping and repainting.'

'There are the damaged plates as well, sir,' Bergman reminded him.

Walther nodded. 'I would have said about seventy-two hours if we were still at Wilhelmshaven. But I doubt if our French friends at the dockyard will be so keen on hard work. Mind you, after what happened at Oran they might welcome the opportunity of hitting back at their former allies.'

'Oran, sir? What happened? I'm a bit out of touch with the news.'

'It was quite a nasty business - even for the British,' Walther explained. 'Apparently Churchill took the view that the French fleet should either scuttle itself or sail to the West Indies and disarm. And he told Darlan so in a few choice words. The French C-in-C had already received a promise from the Fuehrer that Germany would not use any units of the French fleet and, in defiance of the British ultimatum, he recalled all operational warships to France. Churchill was furious. And he sent a British fleet to Oran with orders to blow the French out of the water if they refused to scuttle their ships. I understand that the French suffered a couple of thousand casualties as a result. So I wouldn't say that either Churchill or the Royal Navy were very popular in France right now.'

'So they're helping us in the dockyard?'

'They've got to live,' Walther observed with a shrug. 'Even when his country is occupied by the enemy, the average man must carry on working if he wants to eat. But they're not putting themselves to any inconvenience and we suspect that there are small pockets of Communist saboteurs already working against us. In the circumstances I think we can assume that *UB-44* will be out of action for at least fourteen days. So ten days leave will fit in nicely.'

Bergman put on his cap and saluted. 'I appreciate the suggestion, sir, but a week will be sufficient. I must make sure we have enough time to train the new crew.'

'Very well, Bergman. I'll leave it to you. Enjoy yourself for a few days and make sure you come back fighting fit.'

The streets of Lorient seemed strangely dismal - as if the shame of defeat had snuffed out the spark of life of its inhabitants. Even the dogs looked miserable as they nosed for scraps amongst the garbage cans, with their tails between their legs. Somehow Bergman did not feel like a conquering hero. Not that he wanted to - it was not in his character. But, even so, he had anticipated some feeling of elation.

The excitement on *UB-44*'s bridge when they first

sighted the misty coastline of France was still fresh in his memory. Their rendezvous at Belle lie was within two minutes of Hauptmann's ETA and the minesweeper *M-16*, with a French pilot aboard, had bustled out to greet them. Everyone experienced the same thrill of excitement as the U-boat entered the swept channel leading into the harbour and the sight of the German flag flying on the Custom House gave them a warm glow of patriotic pride.

But, once ashore, the magic of the moment had faded abruptly. The town looked dead and uninteresting. There was no sparkle and no life. The champagne atmosphere of the busy French seaport had evaporated like an uncorked bottle of cheap wine and there remained only the sour taste of the morning after.

The *Kriegsmarine* had taken over the Prefecture over-looking the harbour, and there were already other U-boats tied up alongside the jetty. Bergman recognized Kretschmer's *U-99* and several of his friends' boats but, anxious to make his report to the Flotilla Commander, he had not delayed to chat. And now, worried by the prospect of a new crew, and depressed by the general smell of defeat and shame that hung like a cloud over the ancient port, he quickened his pace as he hurried back to the harbour.

The Frenchmen he passed in the streets looked at him with sullen suspicion as if his uniform branded him as evil. Bergman was puzzled. So far as he could see, the German servicemen in the town were behaving with careful correctness and he could not understand the atti-tude of the local civilians. And when he found them crossing the road in order to avoid walking past him, his puzzlement turned to irritation.

As he turned the corner he caught a glimpse of a

German sailor going into a public telephone booth. The man seemed to be acting furtively and, on an impulse, Bergman walked across the road. Suddenly the door of the booth pushed open and he found himself face to face with *UB-44's Oberbootsmann*. The Coxswain recovered quickly and stiffened to attention.

'At ease, Herzog. If you're going back to the boat I'll let you know the shore leave arrangements.'

The *Oberbootsmann's* face seemed a shade ruddier than usual and Bergman felt sure he could detect a guilty flush in the florid cheeks. What on earth was Herzog doing making a phone call in the middle of an unfamiliar French town? And why not use the special reduced rate system available to all servicemen in the canteens? The Petty Officer seemed to read his mind.

'They must have been thinking of me, sir, when they routed us back to Lorient.' His short laugh sounded suspiciously hollow. 'I used to have a cousin living in these parts before the war. I thought I'd give him a ring and see if he was okay.'

'Any luck?'

There was a strangely complacent expression on Herzog's face as he nodded. 'Yes, sir,' he said enigmatically. 'I was very lucky.'

GRUPPENFUEHRER GORST PUT the phone down thoughtfully. The Gestapo had already settled themselves into Occupied France like obscene vultures gathering for the blood-feast and their office in Lorient was situated in a discreet back street behind the main harbour. Gorst sat tapping his silver pencil on the desk top as he mulled over the information. He looked up at Dorfmann.

'You were serving in Region 6 recently, weren't you?'

Dorfmann, a tall angular man with thin, bloodless lips and quick, searching eyes, nodded.

'That's right - mostly around the Kiel and Wilhelmshaven districts. Keeping an eye on the Navy. Or we would have done if we'd been allowed to get anywhere near them.'

'Good - in that case you'll probably remember this better than me,' Gorst said quietly. A throat wound acquired in the early days of the Nazi movements struggle for power, restricted his voice to a shrill whisper and the vocal disability added a sinister menace to his huge frame. 'Wasn't there some sort of resistance group operating around the northern dockyards and rumours of a U-boat commander being involved?'

'That's right, *Herr Gruppenfuehrer. We* gave them the code name Group Anton - organized by Jewish woman. Yousoff I think the name was. We were about to move in on them in April but someone tipped them off and they got away.'

Gorst nodded encouragingly. 'Carry on, Dorfmann, I'm interested. What about this U-boat commander?'

'We drew a blank there. Apparently someone saw a naval officer call at the Yousoff woman's house but they couldn't identify him. From the description they gave us of his uniform we reckoned he was a submarine captain. Up until then we had just been keeping observation on the group in the hope they'd lead us to something more important - they seemed to be rather more in the way of intellectual dissidents than activists, if you know what I mean. Naturally we reported the mysterious naval officer to Berlin and they took an immediate interest. Within two days we received orders to arrest all known members of the group but, as I said, by the time we got there, our birds had flown. And although we made a lot of enquiries and received the assistance of the *Kriegsmarine* Special Intelligence Branch we never found out who the officer was.'

'In that case, Dorfmann, I think we may be in luck,' Gorst whispered hoarsely. 'I've just received an anonymous tip-off that a certain U-boat commander in the 10th Flotilla has a Jewish mistress - Rahel Yousoff. And my informant also tells me that the man's name is Bergman - *Kapitanleutnant* Konrad Bergman of *UB-44!*

Dorfman whistled. 'Must be the Yousoff woman who was running Group Anton. Well, how do you like that. So Bergmann must be the U-boat officer we've been looking for. What do we do now?'

Gorst's pudgy face developed an additional double chin as he chuckled deep down inside his wheezing throat. 'We do nothing, Dorfmann. The Gestapo has no power of arrest over a naval officer. And this is far too important a matter to be dealt with at provincial HQ level. It will, of course, be passed on to the right quarters. I happen to know that Heinrich Himmler himself is interested. If he can prove that senior officers are involved in treasonable activities Hitler will extend the Gestapo's powers of arrest to the armed forces. And that means that the *Reichsfuehrer*-SS and the *Schutzstaffeln*[3] will control the Third Reich.' He smiled complacently. 'If this information is correct I can see us getting transferred to our Paris HQ if we play our cards right. I've always fancied that.'

Picking up the telephone he dialed the operator and gave her a Berlin number.

Bergman opened his eyes carefully and was relieved to discover that the room had stopped spinning. His mouth tasted like a sewer, his tongue was thick and furry, and his teeth itched. The soft footsteps of a woman whispered across the carpet and the sharp click of the blinds being pulled grated his raw nerve ends with the shock of a pistol being fired two inches from his left ear. The bright sunlight bursting into the room as the shutters lifted stabbed painfully into his eyes and he rolled over and thrust his face into the pillows with a groan.

Where the hell was he? Not on board *UB-44* that was for sure. The pillow was laced with a subtle but unfamiliar perfume. A distinct improvement on the usual smell of stale cabbage water diced with diesel oil. His right hand groped blindly for a landmark. The bed was wide and luxuriously soft and his curiosity was aroused by the warm hollow left by his unknown companion. The stabbing pain caused by the light had developed into a nagging ache and, with a grunt, he rolled over on to his back. He tried delving back into his memory but the effort only made his aching head pulse more violently.

'For Christ's sake shut those bloody curtains.'

There was an obedient swish as the heavy velvet draped closed and the room suddenly darkened. Bergman sighed. But he did not take the risk of opening his eyes. The footsteps whispered across to the bed and the perfume wafted closer. Unable to restrain his curiosity any longer Bergman sat up. And that was when he discovered he was naked.

'Are you feeling better, *cheri?*'

For God's sake - a tart! A bloody French tart. What the hell had he been doing last night. He could vaguely remember the drinking session with Bauer and Hauptmann. But, after that, it was just a blank. They must have ended up in some back-street brothel stoned out of their minds. Yet the voice had none of the harshness Bergman associated with the women he had encountered in the red light district of Hamburg. It was soft and well modulated. No, definitely not the voice of a prostitute. He opened his eyes. And neither was the face.

'You look pretty rough,' she told him sympathetically. 'Can I get you anything?'

Bergman shook his head and his brain rattled about inside his skull like a dried pea in a pod. He settled back carefully on the pillow.

'No - but thanks. I'll be all right in a couple of months or so.' He looked up at her. She was dark-haired and attractive. He put her age at around thirty. 'Where the hell am I?' he asked.

The woman smiled. 'Don't look so worried, *Kapitan-leutnant*. You're quite safe — and I promise you didn't try to rape me.'

It was Bergman's turn to smile. Her nightdress was lying over the foot of the bed and her body was naked underneath the silk negligee. It was only loosely tied at the waist and, as he leaned forward, he could see the firm roundness of her breasts and the dark, hard peaks of her nipples outlined against the thin material.

'Well, I should have done,' he told her. He was surprised by his uncharacteristic brashness. 'I must have been more drunk than I thought if I passed up the chance.'

'You were pretty high,' she agreed. But there was no reproof in the tone of her voice. 'There were four of you at *La Bagatelle*. I think you had been celebrating someone's promotion or something. At any rate you were all fairly far gone. One of your friends - his name was Hermann, I think - wanted to go on to a hotel with some of the girls you'd picked up in a bar somewhere along the line. But you didn't seem too happy at the idea - and I don't blame you having seen the girls you had in tow - so I dived in and rescued you.'

'But why me?'

She shrugged and the negligee slipped lower with the movement of her shoulder to reveal a pertly erect nipple. She pulled the front of the negligee back into place with no sign of embarrassment.

'I don't know. Somehow you didn't look right in those sort of surroundings. I happen to know a few things about sailors.' She looked away suddenly. 'My husband was also a submarine captain - in the French Navy, of course.'

No attempt to probe. He accepted her and let it pass without comment.

'It was very kind of you. I hope I wasn't too much trouble last night.'

'Oh, not the first night. None at all. You just passed out on the bed.'

'You mean this isn't Wednesday?' Christ, thought Bergman, I was worse than I thought.

'No, it's Thursday. You slept the clock around yesterday and I thought it best to leave you. You must have been exhausted.' She smiled at some secret memory. 'Mind you, I wouldn't say you exactly behaved yourself last night.'

'What does that mean?'

'You seemed to be having a sort of nightmare. You kept yelling out that .the water was cold. And you were hammering at the bed with your fists and telling someone to open the hatch. I was beginning to get worried about you. Then you started shivering and saying you were cold and that you were drowning.' She looked at him sharply.

'It wasn't just a dream, either — you really *were* as cold as ice.'

A sudden thought crossed Bergman's mind. But he dismissed it as impossible. And yet, here he was in the bed, and his clothes were neatly folded on the chair by the window.

'How did you know?'

The woman's eyes looked at him softly and she smiled. 'I got in and warmed you up,' she said simply.

MICHELLE REFILLED the coffee cup and pushed it across the table. Bergman was feeling better after a hot shower and he seemed a trifle less vulnerable now that he was fully dressed in his uniform again, It was an idiotic situation having breakfast with a complete stranger whose name he had only discovered an hour previously and yet, for some reason, his usual streak of puritanism was not offended.

Little by little, as they talked over coffee, Bergman gathered a few facts about his unconventional hostess. It seemed that Michelle's husband had died a few months earlier when his submarine, *Le Plongeilr,* had been rammed and sunk in an accident off Toulon. And in an attempt to overcome the loneliness of widowhood she had moved to Brittany where she had taken on work for a French naval charity which provided canteen facilities for lower-deck seamen.

'I expect you're wondering why a French woman is taking such care over a German officer when her country has just been defeated,' she said suddenly.

Bergman shook his head. 'It never crossed my mind,' he told her truthfully. 'I can't see myself in the role of the conquering hero or anything like that. And because you are French it doesn't make you any less of a human being than me. That's not the way I see things. I fight for my country. I don't fight *against* anyone.'

'I know how you feel. Jules had similar ideas. Sometimes I get the feeling that sailors all belong to the same country. Do you know what I mean? Perhaps it's because you all fight a common enemy - the sea.'

Bergman sensed the bitterness behind her words.

'Perhaps it's because the sea *is* our country,' he said. 'I must admit that I tend to regard the sea as my friend - not as my enemy.'

'Will you come and see me again? When you get back from your next patrol. You'll be welcome any time.'

'I don't even know if I'll be returning to Lorient next time.' It sounded ungracious after all she had done for him but he was speaking the truth.

'But I thought this was your new base.'

Bergman sensed danger. Was this why she had picked him up — why she had deliberately selected a U-boat commander instead of a subordinate officer? Suddenly he was on his guard.

'I really must be going. Thank you for all you have done. I promise I will come and visit you if I'm in Lorient again.'

He stood up and Michelle reached out to touch his hand. 'I'm sorry,' she said simply. 'I forgot you are still at war and I shouldn't ask questions. Forgive me?'

'Of course.'

She stood close against him and he kissed her lightly on the lips. But the spell was broken. Fighting back his emotions he reminded himself that he was now in occupied territory where every hand was probably against him. Perhaps she was sincere and it had all been a mistake. But it was a chance he could not take. Turning away abruptly Bergman walked to the door and opened it. It was early afternoon but the streets were still deserted. He glanced up at the number over the door, committed it to memory, and began walking slowly towards the harbour.

He was honest enough to admit that Michelle attracted him. And yet one tiny innocent question had turned him against her. Perhaps there'd been nothing in it. And if there had been surely, as a Frenchwoman, it had been her patriotic duty to gain information against her country's enemy. Duty and patriotism were qualities he could understand. But he, too, had a duty even though his conscience balked at the idea of handing her over to the Gestapo on such a flimsy piece of evidence.

Leaning his elbows on the stone wall of the jetty Bergman stared down at the black sluggish water as he turned the problem over in his mind. It was an ironic situation. A casual and probably innocent question from a woman he scarcely knew and he was ready, almost eager, to have her arrested. Yet he was prepared to do everything in his power to protect Rahel who was actively working to overthrow the Reich. Would there ever come a time when it would be possible to reconcile his deeper emotions with the harsh demands of his profession.

Turning away from the wall he began walking down the jetty to the U-boat pier. Perhaps he should give Michelle another chance - call on her again and see what happened.

Bergman knew he was physically attracted to her and his conscience did not require much persuasion. He shrugged away his doubts. Rahel was probably dead by now anyway.

Bauer was standing on *UB-44*'s deck with his suit-cases packed and ready as Bergman came down the gangplank.

'Where on earth have you been, sir?' he asked anxiously. 'I nearly reported you as missing when you didn't turn up yesterday but Hauptmann insisted he saw you going off with a woman and we thought it might be indiscreet to say anything. Are you alright?'

'Yes, thanks, Number One. I gather I was very well looked after.' He smiled at the memory as he opened the lower conning-tower door. 'How about a farewell drink before you go?'

They dropped down into the control room and passed through No 4 bulkhead into the wardroom. Bergman took a bottle from the locker beneath his bunk and placed two glasses on the table. He poured a measure of liquor carefully into each, handed one to Bauer, and took the other himself.

'Good luck, Hermann. I shall be sorry to lose you.'

'Thank you, sir. Let's hope you have no problems with the new crew.' He lifted his glass. 'To *UB-44* - and many happy memories.'

' *UB-44*.' Bergman tilted his head and swallowed the liquor down.

'You know I'm glad you reminded me,' he said putting the empty glass back on the table. 'I'd forgotten about the crew changes. *UB-44*. will seem like a different boat with all those unfamiliar faces. And I can't say that I relish the idea of going into action with untrained men.'

The heavy curtains parted a few inches and Brunner,

the wardroom steward, poked his head through the opening.

'Begging your pardon, sir, but there's a new officer just come aboard.'

'Show him in, Brunner.' Bergman turned to Bauer. 'Probably your replacement. Want to meet him before you shove off?'

The curtains parted again and a tall, slimly built officer with short cropped blond hair and a thin white scar down his cheek, entered the tiny wardroom, clicked his heels, and raised his arm in the Nazi salute.

'*Oberleutnant* von Eckholdt reporting for duty, sir.'

Bergman made no attempt to return the greeting but held out his hand to the new man.

'Welcome aboard, von Eckholdt. This is *Oberleutnant* Bauer, your predecessor.' Von Eckholdt clicked his heels by way of introduction and bowed stiffly. 'Take a seat and have a drink. What's your poison?'

'Thank you, sir, but I do not drink. The Fuehrer has made it clear that he disapproves of alcohol.'

It was unusual to find a *Kriegsmarine* officer who did not drink and Bergman was momentarily nonplussed. Suddenly he remembered the cigarette box on the table and picked it up.

'Cigarette,' he offered.

'Thank you, *Herr Kapitanleutnant,* but I do not approve of smoking.'

'I hope you approve of women,' Bauer murmured.

'Of course - for breeding, naturally.'

Bergman exchanged glances with Bauer but neither said anything. There was an uncomfortable hiatus for a few moments while Bergman tried to think of something to say.

'What boats have you served in, *Herr Oberleutnant*?'

'I spent six months with the Baltic training flotilla but *UB-44.* be my first operational U-boat, sir. But I'm sure it will not be difficult to pick up the threads again.' He smiled complacently. 'After all, the British are a decadent race and there is no one else left to fight now. I gather it is an easy matter to sink their ships - assuming they've got some left.'

Bergman's jaw sagged incredulously. He could not imagine what he had done to deserve this.

'Where *have* you been serving?' he asked out of curiosity.

'Mostly on Special Duties in Berlin, sir. But don't be alarmed. I know what I am doing.'

'I'm glad to hear so,' Bergman commented drily. 'An old friend of mine, Hans Kirchen, was on SD before the war. And he's now one of our top aces. So there seems some reason for hope.'

Von Eckholdt ignored the sarcasm. 'Yes, I have met him, sir. He has an unfortunate attitude to political matters. Of course I know his father very well - an intimate friend of the Fuehrer and a loyal member of the Party.'

Bauer put his empty glass on the table and stood up. 'I really must be going.' He extended a hand towards his successor. 'Nice to have met you. Best of luck.'

Von Eckholdt took his hand, shook it, and then raised his arm. 'Heil Hitler!'

Bauer flapped his arm in a sheepish acknowledgement, threw a quick, meaningful glance at Bergman, and went out. *UB-44's* skipper screwed the top back on the bottle and returned it to the locker. He was beginning actively to dislike von Eckholdt already. It was time to step on him.

'Number One!'

'Sir?'

'I think I should tell you that we do not use the Party salute on this boat. As members of the *Kriegsmarine* we find the orthodox naval salute to be quite adequate for our purposes.'

'I understand, sir.'

'And another thing. Politics are strictly forbidden on board. We are all German sailors fighting in defence of the Fatherland. And that is sufficient inspiration for our task. Understand?'

Von Eckholdt carefully evaded the point. 'I see you are not wearing the official issue dirk sir,' he parried. 'Do I take it that you do not support the Party?'

Bergman avoided the barbed question with equal skill. 'You obviously have little knowledge of the Navy and its history, *Herr Oberleutnant*,' he said coldly. 'Any officer worth his salt would have recognized that it dates back to the days of the old Imperial Navy. In fact, for your information, it belonged to my father. And he was killed on *UC-115* in 1918.'

'I'm sorry, sir. I did not realize ...'

'And stand to attention when you address a superior officer.'

Von Eckholdt obeyed but there was no mistaking the resentment in his eyes. He was not used to being spoken to in such a manner by *Kriegsmarine* officers whether they were *Kapitanleutnants* or *Grossadmirals*. But this was not the moment to reveal his true colours.

Bergman looked him straight in the eye. 'You are assigned to my boat to do a job and to obey orders. And the sooner you remember that I am your captain, the quicker we will get on together. It does not matter a damn whether I support the Party or not. We both fight under the same flag against the same enemy. And we both, I hope, fight for Germany. The next time you have the temerity to doubt my loyalty to the Fatherland I suggest you keep that fact in mind. Now get up to the transportation depot and find out whether our new intake has arrived. Dismiss!'

Von Eckholdt clicked his heels and began raising his right arm. But he thought better of it when he read the expression on Bergman's face. The immaculate Party salute changed awkwardly in mid-flow and ended in an untidy but orthodox naval acknowledgement.

FIVE

UB-44 shuddered as the heavy seas crashed over her bows and swept green down her foredeck. Venting its fury against the steel plating of the conning-tower the angry ocean hurled a wall of stinging spray high into the air before surging back to gather strength for the next assault.

Bergman's oilskins streamed with water and his sea boots squelched wetly on the deck of the bridge where he was standing watch. Behind him, lashed to the periscope standards by their quick-release Steinback patent belts, the port and starboard lookouts kept their unceasing vigil while further aft, Schoen, the sky-watcher, stared upwards at the fast moving storm clouds. The U-boat wallowed into a trough with a gut-churning lurch and groaned with the effort of straining for the top of the crest that followed.

Keep her head to the sea. That was the secret in heavy weather. Hold her on full power and for God's sake don't let her broach - running with a following sea could be fatal for a craft with the inadequate freeboard of a submarine. It meant a slower dive in an emergency - the head sea tended to keep the bows up but in this sort of weather seamanship was more important than U-boat tactics.

Bergman enjoyed rough weather. There was a majesty to the gale-torn sea that the calms and the long mid-Atlantic swell could not match and he savoured the constant battle with the elements. Most U-boat commanders sought shelter beneath the surface when storm clouds threatened but to Bergman storms were a challenge that had to be accepted and won. If a man could tame the sea on his own terms he had made a friend for life. And the U-boats certainly needed friends in deep waters. As the wind abated and the fury of the waves subsided he allowed himself the luxury of objectivity - a state of mind which, few U-boat captains had time to enjoy.

Despite his initial forebodings, things were not turning out so badly after all. Admittedly he had heard nothing of Rahel since December but, in all honesty, he was not surprised, for in his heart of hearts he felt certain that she was dead. In war man could only have time for the living. And, for the moment, there was always Michelle.

Von Eckholdt had proved surprisingly efficient even though his blind allegiance to the Fuehrer remained a barrier between them. But he handled the men well and, although lacking in experience, he understood the subtle art of U-boat command. The new men, too, were standing up to the rigours of combat operations with commendable stamina. And a succession of easy victories had boosted their morale. Bergman's personal score, with two further patrols behind him, was now within striking distance of the magic 100,000 tons and he derived a grim satisfaction from the knowledge that he was maintaining his place as one of Germany's top aces. But, while he had been lucky, many of his friends and comrades had not.

Poor Hermann Bauer had been lost on his first patrol when his new boat had tangled itself in a British minefield off the North Foreland. His old classmate at the Academy, Georg Ulm, had gone too - depth-charged to destruction by an enemy sloop during an abortive attack on a Southampton-bound convoy. Even the aces were falling. Gunther Prien, killer of the *Royal Oak* in the early days of the war and Bergman's companion on their first operation against the British fleet anchorage at Scapa Flow in 1939, had plunged to the bottom on 7 March 1941 in *U-47* after an attack by the corvettes *Arbutus* and *Camellia*. And now, this morning, scarcely ten days later, Bergman had heard the repeated radio requests from Doenitz's Lorient headquarters to two more of the aces, Schepke and Kretschmer:

U-99 and U-100 report your position ... U-99 and U-100 report your position ...

The ominous lack of response worried him. Ever since his first trip in a TJ-boat in those far-off days before the war Bergman had come to look upon Otto Kretschmer as his mentor and guide. And he had instructed his senior radio operator, Drache, to stay tuned into the 4995 kc/s band for the latest news of *U-99*. It seemed incredible that anything should have happened to Kretschmer - he was probably the greatest U-boat commander of the war - and Bergman felt sure that Otto had more than enough skill and experience to extricate himself from any sort of trouble. Perhaps, he thought hopefully, *U-99*'s radio gear had been damaged. Or perhaps Kretschmer's boat was lying deep to escape surface patrols and had been unable to pick up or reply to *BdU*'s signals.

Of course now that the war had extended into its second year things were changing. The Royal Navy's escort organization was growing daily more efficient and the new ships, the new attack techniques, and the new weapons, were all making life more difficult for Hitler's underwater raiders. But, backed by an ever increasing flow of fresh boats from the dockyards and slips of north-west Germany, Doenitz kept his flotillas one jump ahead of the enemy and the U- boats were still on top.

The 'wolf pack' system was developing well and the new mass tactics reflected considerable credit on their creator. Lone U-boats no longer attacked the heavily defended convoys streaming across the Atlantic in ever-increasing numbers. Having sighted the enemy, the first submarine commander on the scene stalked it by day, and then surfaced at night to radio its position to his comrades. Then, like grey wolves closing in on a dying bear, the other U-boats in the area steered towards the convoy track and, when the Senior Officer judged their numbers suffi-cient, they launched a powerful joint attack that, more often than not, destroyed over half the convoy's strength.

Battle tactics, too, were changing under the threat of Britain's fast growing scientific anti-submarine expertise. Night attacks on the surface were now standard practice, for the Royal Navy's hated Asdic detectors were power-less to locate a U-boat operating on the surface and radar sets were not yet available in sufficient quantities to neutralize the ploy. It was the obvious line to follow but it needed a man of Doenitz's genius to grasp the answer, force his U-boat commanders to follow it when all their instincts warned them to hide below the surface, and push it to a devastating conclusion.

Bergman wiped the spray from his face and brought himself back to the realities of the moment. The sun, a watery yellow disc half obscured by dark scudding storm clouds, was sinking lower on the western horizon and visibility began to fall away as twilight closed in. He leaned over the voice- pipe.

'Stand by control room. All hands to diving stations.'

'Diving stations secured, sir.'

'Take her down to thirty feet.' He turned to the lookouts. 'Clear the bridge.'

There was a roar of water as the sea poured into the tanks through the opened valves and *UB-44* tilted gently by the bows. Schoen, Berker, and Ebeling, slipped out of their safety harnesses and dropped through the upper hatch with unhurried speed. Bergman took a final look around the darkening rim of the horizon, lowered himself on to the ladder, and closed the hatch cover.

'Clutches out. Stop engines. Switches on, group down, half speed both.'

It was Erich Reidel's first trip as a fully-fledged Watch Officer and he kept an anxious eye on the dials as he took *UB-44* to periscope depth. Only a month earlier he had been an insignificant *Fahnrich*[5] and the new responsibilities hung heavy on his young shoulders.

'Lower hatch shut - clips fastened!'

Bergman dropped down into the control room, shrugged off his wet oilskins, and threw them to Brunner. The sea boots thudded into a corner and he checked the dials of the diving table as he pulled on the plimsolls which the steward handed to him.

'Thirty feet and level, sir.'

'Time?' Bergman asked Giesse, the duty coxswain sitting at the diving planes.

'One minute 12, sir.'

Bergman nodded.

'You're doing quite well, Riedel. That's a five second improvement. Think you could make forty-five in an emergency?'

'I'll have a bloody good try, sir.'

'That's the spirit, lad.' Bergman patted his shoulder and glanced at the instruments to recheck his first impressions. 'Any problems?'

'No, sir.'

'Giesse?' Bergman could see from the expression in the duty coxswain's face that he did not agree.

'Starboard 5 tank was slow flooding up, sir. I don't think the valve was fully open.'

Bergman walked across to the line of valve wheels that hung from the overhead bulkhead and examined the wheel controlling the Starboard 5 vent. It was wound down to maximum and was lodged tightly against the safety stop.

'Well, Number Two?'

Riedel flushed. 'It *was* a bit sluggish, sir,' he admitted. 'The panel light came on about five seconds late. I thought it might be some seaweed choking the valve.'

'You could well be right. On the other hand there might be a piece of flotsam jamming it up. Or a mechanical malfunction. Whatever it is it needs checking when we surface. And next time it happens I expect you to tell me - the safety of the boat is my responsibility.'

'I'm sorry, sir.'

'Right - put it down to experience.' Bergman liked the

young officer. He'd got the enthusiasm and potential to be a good captain one day. But the lesson had to be driven home hard. 'Let's assume you reported the matter to me correctly. Have you considered the danger of a sluggish valve?'

'No, sir. We got down okay. So, subject to sorting it out later, I can't see any particular problem.'

'I'll spell it out for you then. If there is a mechanical malfunction the valve will probably stick again when we close the vents and blow the tanks for surfacing. If the vent stays open, the tank will remain flooded and the trim will be upset.' He paused for effect and then asked suddenly: 'What is the capacity of Starboard 5 tank?'

'Six tons, sir.'

'Right - now just imagine what sort of a list we'll have if we come up to the surface with six tons of water on the starboard side. Think about it - and watch it next time.'

Riedel nodded. He knew Bergman was right and he accepted the reprimand in the spirit in which it had been given. But to a young man eager to prove his ability to control a U-boat, it hurt.

Bergman continued his methodical routine check of the control room instruments. He could see Herzog discreetly tucked away in one corner but he ignored him and moved on. The coxswain had been a tower of strength in *TJB-44*'s working-up exercises with the new crew but the barrier of mistrust remained between them although Bergman was forced to admit that there had been no further incidents. But, as a precaution, he had re-scheduled the watches to ensure that he and the Coxswain were never on deck at the same time.

Bergman's sense of self-preservation was instinctive and, since the incident with the flying-boat, it was an ever-present consideration. Perhaps Walther had been right and it had been just a case of *blechkoller*. Time alone would tell. But in the meantime he intended to make sure that Herzog was given no further opportunities to kill him.

Giesse reached up and tugged the cord of the ship's bell eight times to signal the end of the 2nd Dog Watch - 8.00 p.m. *Oberleutnant* von Eckholdt appeared through the rear watertight bulkhead, walked across to the Deck Log, and signed on as Officer of the Watch.

'Good evening, Number One. You should be in for a calm night - the storm seems to be dying down. Surface at four bells and start charging the batteries. Riedel will take over the Middle Watch and I'll be up for the Morning Watch as usual. Any questions?'

'No, sir.'

'Just one other thing. Starboard 5 vent is sluggish so watch it when you surface. Better get a repair party to check it over at the first opportunity.' He stopped to read the log entries, initialed them, and began walking aft. 'Good night, Number One. And let's hope it's a quiet one. I could do with some sleep.'

Riedel was already climbing into his bunk on the port side of the wardroom as Bergman pushed through the curtains. He poured himself some coffee from the vacuum flask and sat down on the leather settee that took up most of the after bulkhead space of their cramped home. Sipping the strong black brew Bergman savoured the flavour. It was good to taste some decent coffee after the *ersatz* acorn grindings that passed for coffee in wartime Germany. It was part of a large consignment confiscated by the *Kriegsmarine* on its way from Brest to Paris. And, for once, *UB-44's* skipper did not despise the spoils of victory. He looked up at the bunk.

'Goodnight, Riedel.'

There was no answer. Riedel was already asleep. Poor little bastard, Bergman thought to himself. Only eighteen years old and holding down a man's job already. And in a couple of years, perhaps even less, he'll be commanding his own boat and killing with the rest of us. Killing? Bergman had long since stopped deceiving himself. All those years of training - of acquiring the skills of seamanship and learning the arts of war. And for what? To become a professional killer. A killer who crept unseen beneath the surface on an unsuspecting victim and struck like an ancient assassin obeying the mystic commands of Hasan, son of Sabah. Was it a coincidence that Hasan's medieval castle was known as the Eagle's Nest and that the Eagle was the symbol of the German Reich? Or that the swastika had its origins in the same Indo-Persian culture.

Taking a magazine down from the rack Bergman looked at it and tried to focus his mind. Lack of concentration was one of the first symptoms of combat fatigue. And this was not the first warning. He must see Walther when *UB-44* got back to Lorient.

It was reassuring to know that Michelle would be waiting for him. She seemed somehow to sense he was returning almost as soon as *UB-44's* bows edged into the swept channel and picked up the outer Main Channel buoy. And by the time he was easing the U-boat into its berth alongside Pier 5 she was already at the harbour wall. Michelle, with the softly yielding body, and an understanding sympathy that followed his changing moods like the sails of a windjammer tacking with the breeze.

Bergman's head dropped forward on to his chest and his eyes closed. Worn out by the physical and mental demands of combat command he fell asleep on the settee and lapsed into a fitful dream in which Michelle and Rahel figured prominently.

'Captain to the control room!'

Von Eckholdt's shout woke him with a start as it boomed through the intercom loudspeaker above his head. He was wide awake and on his feet in an instant. A defiant snore from the upper bunk showed that Riedel remained undisturbed. Bergman smiled. Make the most of it, boy. One day you'll be the captain and from that moment on you won't know the meaning of sleep. Pushing the curtains aside he squeezed through the watertight door into the control room.

'Hydrophone report — HE on starboard bow quarter, sir. The north-east horizon looks darker than normal but my night vision's not as good as it should be.'

Bergman nodded. 'Up periscope!' He glanced across to the hydrophone operator hunched over his sound-detecting gear. 'What's your reading, Schiller?'

Schiller had served with *UB-44 since its* first commission and he knew every detail of Bergman's pre-attack routine. And although the ear-phones clamped to his head cut him off from every sound except those humming through his sensitive listening devices, he knew the question had been asked. He lifted the left pad from his ear as he turned.

'There's a wide arc of sound, sir. At least a mile in length. Mixture of reciprocating and diesel engines. Distance around five miles and moving slowly.'

'A large convoy?'

'Almost certainly, sir.'

Bergman gripped the handles of the periscope as the viewing lenses came level with his eyes. Pushing his face deep into the rubber cups that protected the objectives, he stared into the black world on the surface. And, after a routine sweep of 360° to ensure no ships were danger-ously close, he swung the eye of the 'scope back on to the north-easterly bearing. The moon had not yet risen and it needed the skilled eyes of an experienced seaman to discern the presence of ships. But von Eckholdt had been right. Against the velvet blackness of the night horizon he could just pick out the deeper darkness of objects slowly moving ahead. And, as he watched, he saw a series of short sharp flashes from a shaded blue signal lamp as the convoy commodore called up one of the escorts.

'Group up - full ahead both. Steer 2-7-5.'

'Full ahead both!'

'Steering 2 — 7-5,sir'

'Down periscope.'

The course change brought them on a parallel course to the line of darkened ships and, by increasing to their submerged maximum of 7 knots, *UB-44* skillfully matched the convoy's speed.

Bergman stepped back from the periscope and moved across to the chart table. With Hauptmann gone, the U-boat's navigation had become his responsibility and he bent forward over the chart. The thin pencil line marking their course stopped at 20.00 hours when the watch had changed. And, stretching out from the circled cross of the last fix, a fainter line showed their projected course until midnight when it was the Watch Officer's duty to correct the plot and lay off a new course for the next four hours.

Herzog was already at his side holding the log book. And as Bergman picked up a pencil and a pair of dividers the Coxswain read out the entries.

'20.00 hours. Speed 3 knots - course 240. 21.000 hours course changed to 230 - speed constant. 21-35 hours speed increased to 7 knots and course 275.'

Bergman measured off three nautical miles on a bearing of 240° and ruled a straight line between the two points. Then, placing his circular protractor over the DR fix at 21-00 hours, he lined off a new course to the scale distance for 7 /12ths of three nautical miles. His pencil marked the 21-35 fix and he carefully ruled out their new course of 275 magnetic. He stared down at the chart for a few moments. Then he returned to the periscope. Snapping his finger and thumb sharply he waited for the column to rise up from its well in the floor. The dark smudges were still moving westwards as he checked the convoy's course and speed. Satisfied, he stepped back, and nodded for the periscope to be lowered into its oily womb.

'Drache!'

The radio operator emerged from his compartment abaft the control room with a signal pad ready in his hand.

'Get a signal off to *BdU*. Large convoy sighted in Square MK-409. Course 275 - speed 7 knots. Am shadowing. Will report confirmed course, speed, and position in one hour.'

Drache read back the signal and then hurried aft to his transmitter. Less than a minute later the sharp pulses of his radio message were on their way to U-boat HQ at Lorient.

Bergman stared down at the chart again and called von Eckholdt across. 'I'd say they were about seven miles off on the starboard beam. I doubt if they'll spot us if we surface. And in any case we can't hold maximum under-water speed for too long or we'll drain the batteries. I propose to shadow them until we get some support. *BdU* will advise us who else is in the area.'

'Why not go in now, sir,' the Executive Officer urged. 'If we make the first attack and catch 'em by surprise we could make a real killing.'

Bergman shook his head. 'I disagree, Number One. We've only got nine torpedoes so that means a maximum of nine hits - assuming we're going to perform miracles. There must be a good fifty ships in the convoy. Much better to wait for another couple of boats and launch a concerted simultaneous attack - probably have thirty torpedoes between us. And if we use different bearings we'll confuse the enemy defence and give ourselves more time to get away.' The old instinct for self-preservation was, as always, in the forefront of Bergman's plans. He smiled at his weakness and wondered whether he would ever go mad one day and take a risk.

'Stand by to surface.'

Brunner was holding his oilskins; he thrust his arms down into the sleeves and stepped into his sea boots at the same time. Maas and Galster, the two lookouts, were ready at the foot of the ladder and Herzog, as Duty Coxswain of the Watch, was in the process of climbing into his oilskins. Like hell, thought Bergman. I'm not having that bastard on the bridge with me.

'Belay there, Coxswain. I want you to stay below. The fewer topsides the better. And I shall need someone in the control room to log the course changes so that we can give *BdU* an accurate fix.'

Herzog shrugged off the black rubber cape. Too late to save your skin now, Herr Kapitanleutnant, he told himself. I've done my part. The Gestapo will soon be taking care of you - and your girlfriend. He moved to the diving table, took his place at the 'planes, and waited. His face was completely expressionless.

Bergman stepped on to the ladder and reached up to unclip the lower hatch.

'Take her up, Number One.'

'Close main vents - 'planes to rise. Blow all tanks!'

UB-44's bows lifted as the hydroplanes tilted and a rush of compressed air screamed through the pipes to thrust the sea from the ballast tanks. The depth-gauge needles flickered and began to inch slowly upwards while, between the two dials that dominated the diving table, the hull-shaped symbol of the inclometer mirrored the rising angle of the U- boat.

Bergman twisted the clips securing the hatch and slid them back. Watching the gauges carefully he thrust the lid of the hatch upwards as the red needles touched the 10 feet calibration mark. The ice-cold water that cascaded down through the opened hatch was a routine annoyance and he swore from habit as the first rush drenched him from head to foot. The lower conning-tower compartment of the Type VI IB U-boats was a free-flooding area and there was always a residue of water still swirling about inside as they came to the surface. It soon drained down through the scuppers and it was then merely a matter of scrambling up the ladder to unfasten the upper hatch. But this time it didn't die away into a trickle. It continued at full flood with a force that snatched Bergman's breath away.

Fighting to retain his grip on the ladder as the sea roared down through the opened hatch he knew instinc- tively that something was wrong. But Maas was right behind him, pushing hard in the rush to get to the bridge, and he was being forced forward despite his efforts to retreat. Turning his head to shout a warning, he was rewarded with a mouthful of ice-cold water that left him choking and gasping. And, unable to speak, Bergman kicked down brutally with his boot. Maas took the blow on his shoulder, swayed precariously on the narrow ladder, and thrust up one hand to grip the edge of the hatch and keep his balance. He realized that the skipper was trying to come down again, but with Galster beneath him, he was unable to move in either direction and the roaring flood of black water unnerved him. He shouted to Galster to get down the ladder, but terrified of falling, he continued to grasp the edge of the hatch opening with his right hand as Bergman's heavy sea boots kicked at his shoulders.

Von Eckholdt could not understand what was happening. Staring up at the tangle of bodies clustered on the ladder he watched with frozen horror as the sea flooded down into the control room. Only Herzog - with a veteran submariner's nose for imminent disaster - grasped the situation and, throwing himself at the bottom of the ladder, he grabbed hold of Galster's legs and forced him on to the floor.

'Come on down you stupid bastard!' he yelled at Maas. But, petrified with terror, the young seaman clung on tightly and refused to move.

Von Eckholdt, quickly recovering from the initial shock, summed up the danger of the situation.

'Close all watertight doors! Get the pumps going! Giesse - take over the controls and put the 'planes amidships. Stop blowing!'

Doubling himself into a ball so that he could squeeze

out of the hatch, but still hampered by the terrified Maas crouched on the ladder directly beneath him, Bergman reached up, grabbed the handle of the hatch cover, and pulled it down hard. The salt water had completely blinded him, but he carried out the operation automatically as his reflexes responded to the danger. The heavy steel hatch cover slammed down with a thud and Maas's sudden shriek of agony echoed round the walls of the control room.

Wiping the water from his eyes Bergman looked up to see the stumps of two fingers jerking spasmodically where the sharp steel edge of the hatch cover had chopped through the bone and amputated them as cleanly as a surgeon's knife. Blood was pouring down Maas's trapped hand. Swallowing back the bile in his mouth Bergman reached up for the clips again.

'Hold him while I try to free the hatch. And get Steiner into the control room at the double.'

Herzog joined the skipper on the ladder and clamped his massive arms around Maas, forcing him back against the steel rungs to hold him steady, while Bergman heaved the heavy cover upwards to free the mangled hand. The weight of the sea pressing down on top of the hatch lid made it difficult to lift and he was in an awkward doubled-up position that prevented him from using his strength to its best advantage.

Putting his shoulder against the cover Bergman pushed hard. It lifted slightly and then slammed shut again. The extra pain was more than Maas could endure. He screamed again and fainted. Bergman thrust again, and this time it raised sufficiently for Herzog to pull the seaman clear. Then it settled back into its seating with a thud and Bergman secured the clips.

Steiner was already bending over the unconscious lookout as Bergman came down the ladder. The needle of the hypodermic stabbed into the man's arm and the *Sanitsasobermaat* looked up as he withdrew the syringe.

'Two fingers gone, sir,' he told Bergman. 'And I'll have to amputate the other two - there's no hope of saving them.' The *Kapitanleutnant* nodded. It did not require much medical knowledge to see that the fingers could not be saved.

'Take him to the wardroom. You can operate on the table. And let me know if you need anything. When you've finished put him in my bunk.'

Bergman turned to von Eckholdt as Maas was gently carried out through the aft watertight door. The pumps were working steadily to clear the water on the floor of the control room and two of the seamen were busy drying up with long- handled mops.

'What happened, sir? Did you open the hatch while we were still submerged?'

Bergman shook his head. He pointed to a small dial on the control panel above the diving table.

'That's the answer, Number One. I suppose it was my fault for not noticing it earlier. We were surfacing with a 7° list to starboard. One side of the conning-tower was clear of the sea but the other was scooping it up through the drain holes. It's that bloody valve on Starboard 5 tank.'

'What happens now, sir?'

'I propose to restore trim by counter-flooding and proceed with our standard surfacing routine,' Bergman told him grimly. He turned to Giesse. 'Flood Port 5 tank.'

The Duty Coxswain reached up to turn the valve wheel and waited for the green light to come on.

'Port 5 flooded, sir.'

'Right - now keep port and starboard 5 tanks flooded up but blow all the others. 'Planes to rise. Stand by to surface.'

Galster closed up behind the skipper as he climbed the ladder and Lutz brought up the rear as replacement for the injured Maas. This time the lateral stability indicator remained steady and *UB-44* rose smoothly on an even keel.

'Ten feet!' Giesse reported.

Bracing himself against the sudden rush of ice-cold water Bergman took a deep breath, pulled the clips, and thrust the steel cover upwards. The dark cavern of the lower compartment smelled damp and salty but, riding clear of the surface, the scuppers had already drained most of the sea away and only a harmless trickle remained to dribble down through the opening. With a sigh of relief he swarmed up into the gloomy vault and started climbing the second ladder.

The stars swayed gently over Bergman's head as he threw back the top hatch and hauled himself on to the bridge. The weather was clearing rapidly after the storm and the moon was due to rise in less than an hour. Galster and Lutz hurried to their lookout positions while the skipper searched the horizon with his nightglasses. He could pick out the dark shapes of the convoy against the northern horizon and it was obvious that, cloaked by the storm clouds on their stern quarter, the U-boat was invisible to the escorts.

'Transfer control to bridge. Obey telegraphs.' He waited for the order to be repeated back. 'Switches off - shut down motors. Start engines. Clutches in-half ahead both.'

The repeater bell of the telegraph pinged faintly deep

down in the engine room and the exhausts coughed softly back to life as the engineers tried to keep the noise down to avoid alerting the enemy.

'Sextant to the bridge, Number One.'

UB-44 cruised softly at half speed as she maintained course parallel to the convoy and it seemed somehow unreal to the men on the bridge to remain so relaxed when the enemy was in sight. Bergman was staring up at the black vault of the sky as von Eckholdt handed him the sextant.

'Thank God the storm's cleared, Number One. All we need are a couple of good star sights and Doenitz will be able to pinpoint the convoy on his charts to within half a mile.' He smiled wryly. 'I doubt if the DR position we reported earlier will have been much use to him.'

Putting the sextant to his eye Bergman located Betelgeuse and called off the angle to the Executive Officer who scribbled the figures down in his note pad. Swinging to the left, he picked up a second constellation, selected the prime star of the group, and sighted it carefully in the bubble. Then, satisfied, he handed the instrument back to von Eckholdt and resumed observation on the convoy as the Executive Officer hurried below to plot UB-44's correct position from the star tables.

The enemy ships were still moving at a steady seven knots and Bergman estimated the size of the convoy as upwards of fifty ships plus escorts. A sizeable target by any standards. Suddenly, as he watched, the dark mass turned northwards and he saw one of the escorts sweep astern of an old coal- burning freighter shepherding it on to the new course. He gauged the alteration by eye and leaned forward over the voice-pipe.

'Helmsman - steer four points to starboard.'

UB-44's bows swung in response to the rudder but Bergmann realized that, turning on the outer circle, he was losing ground.

'Full ahead both!'

The U-boat surged forward to close her position and, within minutes, she was snugly back on station, six miles on the port beam of the convoy.

'Half speed ahead. Helm 'midships. Steady as she *goes?*

The white bow wave fell away and the diesels reverted to their low throbbing rumble as *UB-44* throttled back to match the convoy's funereal speed. There was still no indication that they had been spotted by the escorts and Bergman lowered the binoculars and rested his elbows on the rim of the conning-tower screen.

'I've fixed the new position, sir,' von Eckholdt reported as he climbed back to the bridge. 'We were 22 miles SW of our DR position but I've corrected the plot and Herzog is noting all course changes and speeds. Riedel's marking the chart.' 'So he's got up then?'

'Not much chance of sleeping while Steiner's using the wardroom as an operating theatre - poor little bastard looked as sick as hell when he came into the control room. It must be enough to turn anyone up seeing a couple of nice neat fingers lying out on the table like a pair of sausages ready for breakfast.'

'How is Maas?' he asked.

'Sleeping. Steiner thinks he'll be okay.'

Okay. Bergman stared out to sea without speaking. The banal inadequacy of the two syllables made mockery of the hopes that lay behind them. He knew every man on board *XJB-44*; their service career, their qualifications, their family backgrounds, their life histories. Every U-boat captain took the same interest in his men. And Maas? He'd been a student at the Berlin Music Acadamy before his conscription into the *Kriegsmarine*. And what good was a musician with no fingers on his right hand ...

Von Ekholdt suddenly broke into his thoughts. 'I've been thinking, sir. If the convoy is sailing on a westerly course I presume most of the ships will be in ballast. There doesn't seem much point in sinking empty vessels in an outward bound convoy. Perhaps we should scout around and look for a well-laden group.'

'I'll wait for Doenitz's orders, Number One,' Bergman told him. 'But I would suggest you are less scathing about empty ships in the future. Remember that the enemy cannot afford to lose any ships - laden or unladen. Naturally it is better to sink a ship that's carrying cargo. But that is not our primary operational task. Our purpose is to strangle the British seaborne supply lines and that means we must sink every ship we see. It leaves the enemy with one less bottom in which to carry cargo next time.'

Von Eckholdt shrugged. He saw the U-boat war in much more dramatic terms and, like many Nazi fanatics, he failed to grasp the inevitable boredom that made up ninety-nine per cent of the war at sea. It was a state of mind that caused Raeder and his senior staff officers many uneasy moments as they sought to parry the Fuehrer's grandiloquent schemes for maritime victory. It was an uphill struggle but, while they could keep Hitler's meddling hands off the higher direction of naval operations, they were quietly confident of achieving victory for Germany.

'I'm going below to signal *BdU*,' Bergman told him. 'Stay on watch until I relieve you. Keep a constant position on the convoy and don't try to be clever. If the escorts spot us you are to dive immediately.'

The Executive Officer's expression was fortunately hidden in the darkness. Picking up his night glasses he took over the task of watching the convoy ...

SIX

Vice Admiral Karl Doenitz leaned forward across the vast operational chart depicting the North Atlantic battle area and stared down at the two red counters marking the last reported positions of *U-99* and *U-100*. He had been in conference at his Paris headquarters in the Avenue Souchet when the first news that Kretschmer and Schepke had failed to make their routine radio calls had been received. And, bringing the meeting to an abrupt close, he had sent for his staff car to take him back to Lorient.

Now, twenty-four hours later, there was still no news and the hollow greyness of the Vice Admiral's face reflected the strain and tension of a sleepless night.

'Signal from *UB-44*, sir'

Doenitz took the slip of paper and read it. With a final glance at the two red counters he turned away from the chart. Kretschmer and Schepke would have to wait. He handed the signal to Luderitz, the Duty Staff Officer, and watched as the red counter marked *UB-44* and the white counter representing the convoy were slid into place on Square MK-409.

'What do we have in the area, Luderitz?'

The Staff Kapitans expert eye ran across the squared board and he consulted the papers in his hand.

'UB-203 and U-102 could be there before dawn, sir. And we might get another two boats into the area by sunset tomorrow. We're a bit thin on the ground and it would mean calling off the hunt for the east-bound convoy.'

Doenitz rubbed his chin thoughtfully. The east-bound convoy was already severely mauled. Lemp, the man who had sunk the *Athenia* on the first day of the war, had picked it up and shadowed it in *UB-110* and both Schepke and Kretschmer had ripped into the group of almost defenceless ships like ravaging lions attacking a herd of docile sheep. *Ferm, Bedouin, France Comte, Venetia,*]. *B. White* and *Korsham* had all been sent to the bottom in a dramatic night battle and the staff of *BdU* had exchanged grins of self-satisfied triumph as each sinking was reported. The remains of the shattered convoy were now streaming towards Britain

- demoralized and bewildered by the fury of the U-boat's sudden attack. But scattered. That was the significant point -
- scattered. Which meant that further attacks would be limited to single ships. And, to Doenitz, piecemeal attacks on solitary vessels were uneconomic. Better in the circumstances to leave the convoy's fate in the hands of the Luftwaffe.

Of course the group of darkened ships moving west-wards would be sailing in ballast. But in a few week's time they would be returning, fully laden, to feed more desperately needed material into Churchill's hungry war machine. Well, better today than tomorrow. It was tonnage that counted. Destroy more ships than Britain could build and the war was as good as won. Doenitz turned on his heel as he made his decision.

'We attack the convoy reported by *UB-44*,' He told Luderitz. 'Call up *UB-203* and *U-102*. And advise Bergman to commence attack at midnight.'

'Do you want the other two boats as well, Vice Admiral?'

'No. Route them eastwards to pick up the remains of *U-110*'s convoy. I'm confident that the three boats in the area will cope.'

He looked up as a young flag-lieutenant pushed through the swing doors of the Operations Room and saluted. His face was white with shock and Doenitz knew that he was bringing bad news.

'Kretschmer?' Somehow he knew it must be.

Oberleutnant Hirschfeldt nodded. 'Yes, sir. The wireless room has just monitored a signal from the enemy destroyer *Walker* to the British Admiralty. It's been decoded, sir.'

The Commander-in-Chief, U-boats, took the paper and read it quickly. There were several blanks where German Intelligence had failed to break the cypher but the message was starkly clear. Doenitz passed his hands across his face. Then he straightened up and walked across to the Plotting Officer at the Operations table.

'Remove *U-99* and *U-100* from the board, Amsbach,'

he told the Duty Commander. 'They won't be any use to us now.'

The harshness of the order was no more than a statement of unalterable fact but it served to hide his emotion. Doenitz counted Kretschmer amongst his personal friends and the Navy could ill-afford to lose men of his quality and integrity. And neither could Germany. As Amsback scooped the two red counters from the board like a croupier raking in the losing stakes in the aftermath of a roulette game, the Vice Admiral turned wearily to the Duty Captain.

'It was one of those damned British escort groups - we identified *Walker* as the group leader's ship a few months ago. Must have been operating independently of the convoy but within call. Both our boats have gone to the bottom. Schepke is dead. And so far as I can gather Kretschmer has been taken prisoner together with most of his crew. You'd better warn *UB-44* that there's an escort group in the vicinity - I can't afford to lose Bergman as well.'

Luderitz scribbled a signal and handed it to the runner to take to the wireless room for coding and transmission.

'How do you account for the enemy's sudden run of success, sir?' he asked.

'Science and guts, *Herr Kapitan*. The Royal Navy has the guts and British science has perfected the art of radio location. They can now spot us on the surface with radar as well as locating us below the surface with asdic. It makes things very difficult for our commanders at sea. And the real danger is that, sooner or later, they'll be building compact radar sets suitable for use in aircraft and when they do, the U-boat as we know it is doomed.'

Doenitz sighed. Walking across to a side table he poured himself some *ersatz* coffee. It tasted bitter and unpleasant, but with characteristic selflessness he had issued orders that gave operational U-boats first call on all stocks of fresh coffee confiscated from French ware-houses. So far as the Vice Admiral was concerned, no sacrifice was too great if it helped the men fighting for Germany in the underwater war.

'And we can thank our friend Goering for this mess,' he continued bitterly. 'Do you realize that we were ahead of the British in radar development in 1939? Our 80cm *Seetakt* sets were the best in the world — but they were too damned big for use in U-boats or aircraft. We could have followed along the lines the enemy took up - smaller and smaller waves - until we perfected the 9cm sets the British are now using against us. But that fool Goering told the Fuehrer we should close-down any line of research that could not produce positive results within six months because, by then, the war would be over. And Hitler believed him.'

Doenitz swallowed the remains of his coffee and threw the paper cup into a convenient waste bin with a violent gesture of disgust.

'But is there no way we can overcome the enemy's advantage?' Luderitz asked anxiously.

The Vice Admiral's eyes twinkled suddenly. 'There is indeed, *Herr Kapitan*,' he said enigmatically. 'In fact that is precisely what the Avenue Souchet conference was about. And I think we may have come up with the answer.' Doenitz picked up his gold peaked cap. 'It's a long drive to Paris and I must get back to tie up the loose ends. You can expect me sometime tomorrow evening. We've got to pull something out of the hat to compensate for the loss of Prien, Kretschmer, and Schepke. So let's pray that Bergman is successful.'

Luderitz escorted his Chief to the door and accompanied him down the narrow concrete corridor past the *Kriegsmarine* sentries guarding the entrance. They stopped in the shadow of the eight-feet-high blast wall and looked up at the stars as they waited for the Vice Admiral's Mercedes limousine to arrive.

'Reminds me of my days in *UB-68* during the last war,'

Doenitz mused quietly as he picked out the familiar navigational stars swinging high up in the night sky. 'You know I'd give my right arm to be up on the conning-tower with Bergman tomorrow evening. Those young U-boat captains don't know how lucky they are.'

POURING himself another coffee Bergman took it across to the wardroom table and settled down to check through the night's signals for the third time.

Maas was sound asleep in the lower bunk with his heavily bandaged hand resting on a neat steel frame on top of the blanket. Steiner had been making a routine visit every thirty minutes and his prognosis grew more optimistic with each report. Bergman was relieved. *UB-44*'s combat casualty rate was unenviably high and if Maas survived it would be a fillip to morale. He was glad, too, for Steiner's sake.

The young *Sanitatsobermaat* was keen and enthusiastic. A second-year student in Munich in 1939 he had been shoveled into the Nazi war machine without thought to the future. Yet, one day, Germany would need the services of trained doctors and it seemed such a terrible waste to fritter away the potential of men like Steiner in minor medical appointments. Steiner would make a fine doctor one day - if he beat the odds and survived the war. Despite his lack of experience and his rudimentary knowledge of surgery he had carried out the amputation with the skill and care that Bergman normally associated with a trained surgeon. And although the injury might prevent Maas from following his chosen profession he could at least thank the *Sanitatsobermaat* for leaving him with a fingerless hand instead of a stump at the wrist.

Draining the coffee cup Bergman stood up, stretched his cramped muscles, and made his way back to the control room.

'Battery charging completed, sir,' Riedel reported, 'And I've marked off our corrected course.'

Bergman examined the chart carefully. Riedel had plotted every course change with meticulous care and the penciled plot reflected the zig-zag track of the convoy with mirror like accuracy. It wandered across the chart like a demented serpent but, to the trained eye, the trend of its ultimate direction was crystal clear. It was moving west. The *Kapitanleutnant* walked slowly round the control room checking the various instruments and gauges with eyes that, although tired, missed nothing. There was ample oil in the bunkers for another eleven days and *UB-44* still had its full kit of torpedoes. In fact, the future augured well.

'Has the Starboard 5 valve been cleared, Number Two?'

Riedel nodded. 'Yes, sir. The repair party came down about three hours ago. Just a bit of driftwood jamming it. Functioning correctly now, sir.'

Just a bit of driftwood, Bergman reflected. Yet it had nearly caused a disaster and it had cost one man the fingers of his right hand. Picking up the sextant he made his way to the bridge. Convoy HR-15 was still positioned on the starboard beam and von Eckholdt had maintained range precisely as ordered. So far so good. But there were still twenty-four hours to go and there was still plenty of time to make mistakes. He glanced down at the bow wave.

'Have we reduced speed?'

'Yes, sir. The enemy have fallen back to five knots - I think a couple of ships are having engine trouble and they're trying to keep together.'

'Well let's hope they don't speed up during the day or it will throw all our calculations out.' He lifted the sextant to his eye. 'There's only an hour until dawn and I want to get another fix to confirm our position. Then we'll run up to full speed and try to get ahead of the enemy so that he catches us up while we're submerged. This shadowing business is a bit of a cat-and-mouse game. Ever done any before?'

'No, sir.'

'We have to stay out of sight at periscope depth during the daylight hours and as our maximum submerged speed is usually less than the convoy average, it means we start falling behind. So, every now and again, we have to sweep down over the horizon, come to the surface, and then run at full speed to overtake it. Then we vector in again below surface to check that they're still maintaining their mean course.'

'Supposing we've misinterpreted their probable track, sir,' von Eckholdt asked.

'In that case we lose them,' Bergman shrugged. 'But by that time we would normally have several U-boats in the general area and at least one of them will spot it and beam us in. It's the only way we can escape detection from their asdic and radar devices. But if they've got air cover we don't stand much chance of success. A patrol aircraft can force a U-boat to remain submerged well beyond the surface horizon and by the time it can come up again, the convoy has disappeared into the blue.'

He read off two star sights, jotted the angles on a pad, and noted the time of observation. Then, after a final glance at the convoy, Bergman bent over the voice-pipe.

'Full ahead both - and keep it *pianissimo.*'

'*Molto beni, Herr Kapitan,*' chuckled Kohn as he passed the message on. Keep exhaust noise to a minimum. Even if the convoy escorts can't see us they could hear us.

UB-44 gathered speed and began to draw ahead of the enemy ships moving slowly westward on the horizon.

'*BdU* have called up two more boats and I anticipate a combined attack tomorrow night,' Bergman told the Executive Officer. 'I expect to get the go-ahead during the day. And, by the way, there's an escort group operating in the area so we can't afford to take risks.'

He leaned his elbows on the lip of the conning-tower coaming and stared down at the sea. He remained almost motionless and lost in his private thoughts for over thirty minutes and only returned to life when von Eckholdt drew his attention to the first pink streaks of dawn rising astern in the east. He nodded and straightened up.

'Carry on, Number One. I'm going below for breakfast. Steer 2-o-o and stay down for half an hour. It should be safe to surface by then. I want you to hold a parallel course to the convoy at half speed - but keep your eyes skinned for aircraft. I'll come up and relieve you in four hours.'

Bergman slid down the vertical steel ladder as von Eckholdt gave the first stand-by orders for diving. The men in the control room were functioning with their usual efficiency and he noted that Herzog had relieved Giesse at the hydroplane controls although he didn't see any significance in the change of duties.

'Take it easy, lads,' he cautioned as he stopped to check the chart. 'We've got another eighteen hours to go yet.' He handed Riedel the slip of paper on which he had noted the star sights and told him to check their fix. Then he squeezed through the watertight door and poked his head into *UB-44's* diminutive radio cabin.

'Any signals?'

Wolfe looked up from the cypher machine, scribbled one final word on the pink flimsy, and passed it across.

'Just come in, sir.' He grinned. 'Careful - the ink's still wet!'

Bergman scanned the decoded signal quickly:

05-50. ig-3-41. BdU to CO UB-44

Target confirmed. Attack 25-59 tonight. UB-203 and U-102 will support. Strike bearing south. Good luck. Doenitz. BdU.

So that was it. Doenitz obviously agreed that the empty west-bound convoy which von Eckholdt had scorned was worth a three-pronged U-boat attack. And it was good to know they'd be operating with Kirchen's *UB-203*. Elis friendship with Hans dated back to the Naval Academy although, recently the heavy demands of the U-boat service had prevented them from meeting for over six months. And now Doenitz was throwing them together again - in the middle of the Atlantic Ocean!

Pushing the curtains aside he entered the wardroom and sat down at the table. Brunner's choice of menu was never very inspired, and once the stores were reduced to cans, he had a perfect excuse for the lack of variety. But, breakfast at least had one consolation - fresh eggs. And Bergman smiled with anticipation as he savoured the reeking smell of hot fat from the galley.

The rumbling roar of the diesels died away and the deck plating vibrated softly as the motors took over. Bergman could hear the muffled orders of the diving routine through the stout steel wall of the watertight bulk-head that divided the wardroom from the control room and he felt *UB-44* gently as she nosed beneath the waves. Pushing the plate away with a yawn he stood up. Maas was snoring peacefully in the lower bunk and the *Kapi-tanleutnant* heaved himself up to the top berth as quietly as possible to avoid disturbing him. He was asleep almost as soon as his head touched the pillow.

Bergman was still wearing his sea boots, oil-skin trousers, and heavy sweater but he rarely removed these when *UB- 44* was on combat patrol. Enemy counter-attacks usually came without warning and allowed no time for dressing. His face itched with five day's growth of beard and he smelled of BO. But no one else noticed it. Lack of hygiene was an accepted discomfort of the U-boat service and at least everyone else smelled as bad.

'Captain to the control room!'

Bergman's eyes opened immediately and his legs swung over the edge of the bunk in an automatic reflex action. He glanced at the brass-rimmed clock on the wall and swore. His precious chance of sleep had lasted for only twenty minutes.

'Large group of ships approaching, sir. Bearing approximately due north.'

'Up periscope!'

Pushing his eye against the rubber cup Bergman peered through the lens. Apart from a thin mist lingering on the surface, visibility was excellent and the cold blue light of dawn had already extended the horizon to eight miles. Von Eckholdt was right. A convoy was bearing down on them.

'Down periscope.' He stepped back as the squat column slid into its well in the floor. 'Take her to 100 feet.'

'Planes hard a-dive!'

Bergman watched the needles of the gauges drop. 'Planes amidships! Slow ahead both. Rig for silent running.'

The vibrations from the electric motors faded away and a strange stillness settled over the U-boat as it hung suspended in the green void between surface and ocean bottom creeping slowly forward at 2 knots. The men moved quietly, speaking in whispers, and the only sound that could be heard was the wheezing grunt of the pump clearing the bilges. Bergman leaned across to Schiller sitting hunched intently over his listening devices.

'What HE?' he asked.

Schiller cocked his head as his sensitive ears analysed the sounds filtering through the head-phones. 'Same as before, sir.' He sounded puzzled. 'Mixed engine noises and a lot of ships. I'd say it was a convoy - speed around 5 knots.' ' Bergman glanced up at the gyro repeater. He frowned. How could it be? He'd plotted the convoy course for over eight hours and, despite the many varia-tions of its complex zig-zag track, he knew it was heading west. So where the hell did this south-bound group spring from? He turned back to the hydrophone operator.

'Are you sure you've got diesel and reciprocating HE?' 'Yes, sir. Quite positive.'

Bergman stood back rubbing the coarse stubble of his chin. It could be the escort group *BdU* had warned him of but it seemed unlikely that they'd be travelling at five knots. And anyway the HE was all wrong. Added to which he was quite sure he'd identified merchant ships through the periscope. Yet how could it possibly be the same convoy *UB-44* had shadowed the previous night? It didn't make sense.

He sat down on the old canvas seat reserved for his use in the corner of the control room adjacent to the chart table and tried to think. The gyro compass indicated the correct course. And that meant that von Eckholdt had put the U- boat on to the new track as ordered. Bergman sensed someone moving just outside his field of vision and he spun round suddenly to see Herzog moving away from the gyro compass cabinet. Getting up from his seat with unexpected speed, Bergman reached the compass in two rapid strides. 2-0-0. He frowned. Digging back into his memory he could vaguely recall a subconscious impression that *UB-44* had changed direction within the last 30 minutes.

'Have you altered course recently, *Steurmann?* Dichter broke his concentration and looked up from the strip of glass that covered the gyro compass repeater.

'I had to *correct* the course, sir. When I made the usual routine check of the gyro against the magnetic compass it was almost 120° out of true. So I reset it and altered course back to 2 - 0 - 0.'

'That's right, sir,' Riedel confirmed. 'I was standing behind Dichter when he found the error. I'd say it was about 25 minutes ago.'

Bergman nodded. Dichter had been his senior helmsman for eighteen months. He knew he could rely on him. But why should the bloody gyro start playing up now? A sudden suspicion crossed his mind and he moved across to the angled mirror of the periscope system through which they checked the magnetic compass on top of the bridge when they were submerged. It was missing!

Instinctively he turned to Herzog who was seated at his usual station in front of of the hydroplane controls - his eyes fixed intently on the depth-gauges to ensure they were riding at a constant depth.

'What were you doing by the helm a few minutes ago?' Bergman demanded in a whisper.

'Checking the course, sir.'

'Why? Your job is at the diving table. Dichter is responsible for the steering.'

Herzog grinned insolently. 'You know me, sir,' he whispered hoarsely. 'I always like to check things for myself in case of mistakes.'

The whispered voices added a touch of farce to the grim dialogue. Bergman wanted to shout in anger but with the possibility of enemy hydrophones listening on the surface it would have been an invitation to suicide. He could feel the blood pulsing in his neck as he bottled up his rage. Then he saw the gleaming steel spanner lying on a ledge alongside the gyro cabinet.

"Where did that come from?' he demanded.

Herzog looked at it with casual innocence. "I was checking a valve control seating earlier on, sir. Must have forgotten to put it away.'

Bergman turned away abruptly. Choking back his anger he dropped into his canvas chair. He was in no doubt that Herzog had deliberately wedged the spanner into the gyro mechanism to jam the gimbals and cause it to spin erratically - precess was the technical term. And then, after Dichter corrected the gyro error following his routine hourly check of the magnetic standard compass, the Coxswain had removed the prism so that future errors could not be discovered. So, either Dichter had been steering a false course for nearly thirty minutes or, and it was just as bad, they'd been deviating in various directions for an unknown period. Whatever the correct answer might be, the carefully maintained DR plot on the chart was now wildly inaccurate. It had been a very knowledgeable piece of sabotage. Herzog had struck again and, as before, there was not one iota of evidence except his own suspicions.

Pinned down below the surface, steering a course that could be north, south, east, or west, and unable to check the gyro reading against the magnetic compass, UB-44. edged its way through the trackless depths of the ocean like a blind man feeling his way across an open field in a thick fog. And that was not all.

With no means of determining direction Bergman could not be sure if the convoy was holding its original westerly course or whether it had turned south. And it was also possible that he had chanced to cross the path of an entirely different convoy whose presence he had not previously suspected. Of all the cock-ups Bergman had encountered in the course of his career this was the greatest ever.

The pounding beat of massed propellers was now clearly audible inside the U-boat as the convoy closed the range.

'Stop motors! Absolute silence!'

Bergman was not only concerned with the safety of

UB- 44. Much more was now at stake. If the enemy picked up the sounds of a U-boat the whole ambush operation would be put in jeopardy. The convoy would take evasive action by means of an unexpected course change and the escort group lurking somewhere over the horizon would be whistled up for the kill. And if the enemy did not maintain the mean speed and course he had reported to *BdU* not one of the three U-boats would be within attack range that evening.

It was like sheltering in a stuffy tin shed waiting for a thunderstorm to pass overhead but Bergman showed no outward signs of strain or tension as he listened to the approaching thump of engines. It took the convoy over fifteen minutes to pass over the motionless U-boat and then, like the dying sounds of a military band marching down the hill, the engine noises faded and died into the distance.

What now? Bergman wondered whether he dared risk surfacing so that he could check the magnetic compass and grab a sun-sight to establish their correct position. Certainly no new facts on the convoy's course could be signaled back to Doenitz until he knew that the gyro was functioning correctly. Any error in his report would mean an abortive rendezvous with his two companions on a mockingly empty ocean at midnight. It was a chance that had to be taken. 'Stand by to surface. Group down - half ahead both.' *UB-44* began moving slowly ahead as the power came on and von Eckholdt took the crew through the familiar surfacing routine.

'Stop her at thirty feet, Number One.'

Bergman watched the needle of the depth-gauge as if trying to push the self-doubts from his mind by concentrating on the immediate task in hand.

'Thirty feet, sir. Trimmed level.'

'Up periscope!'

Lutmann moved the lever of the hydraulic controls and the column slid smoothly into position as Bergman took his place at the eye-piece. Once round the horizon. All clear. Now the sky search. He flipped the hand lever and the prisms tilted upwards to scan the sky. Okay ... okay ... *damnation!*

'Down periscope!'

He stepped back and turned to von Eckholdt. 'There's a Catalina scouting on the southern horizon - probably bringing up the rear of the convoy. We'll have to lie low for a while.'

In his mind's eye Bergman carried a memory of the sun's position relative to the fore-and-aft line of the U-boat. It was rough and ready but it was better than nothing. He glanced up at the control room clock and then walked over to Dichter to check the gyro repeater. So far as he could judge the reading was accurate to within ten degrees. Which meant the convoy must have been moving south even though it was now out of sight over the horizon. Or, he corrected himself, *a* convoy was moving south — whether it was the group they had shadowed the previous night or another was anybody's guess at the moment.

The inspiration that led him to check their direction relative to the position of the sun had revived his confidence and a new idea was beginning to take root in his mind.

'Up persicope.'

Bergman stooped slightly as he squinted through the lens. He picked up the dark dot of the flying-boat on the horizon and watched it carefully for a period. Then he swung the periscope round to check the sun again. The bright glare in the lens blinded him momentarily but the angle of bearing was enough to confirm his inspired guess - the Catalina was flying eastwards. And the odds were that the convoy was following the same course.

'Steer 0-9-0.' The gyro was steady now and, even if it was inaccurate, it could still be used as a reference for steering directions. 'Full ahead both.'

The vibrating whine of the electric motors rose in pitch and the submarine threshed forward, thrusting the water away with her cold black snout, like an avenging shark.

'Take over the watch, Riedel. And keep her steady at thirty feet. Von Eckholdt - conference in the wardroom, please.'

Bergman pulled the heavy curtains across although their privacy was more imagined than real, due to the presence of Maas in the lower bunk. 'Are you a gambling man, Number One?'

The Executive Officer shrugged. 'Not as a rule, sir.'

'Neither am I - but I've had a crazy idea and I'm prepared to stake my whole professional career on it.' Bergman sat down on the settee and rested his elbows on top of the table. 'It's my guess that the ships we intercepted and shadowed last night were part of a fully-laden eastbound convoy that had been diverted because of Kretschmer's attack on the preceding group. It was turned around to confuse any other U-boats that spotted it and, once the Escort Group was able to report that it had destroyed U-99 and U-100, it was routed back on to its original course. Well?'

Von Echoldt caught Bergman's mood of excitement.

'It's certainly a long shot - but I suppose it's possible, sir. And it must be fairly important if it's got air cover.'

'Precisely. If only that damned gyro hadn't let us down.' Bergman did not intend to reveal his suspicions about Herzog to the Executive Officer. 'As it is we can only make an intelligent guess.'

'It's a hell of a gamble, sir.'

'It is. But I'm prepared to play my hunches. Are you with me?'

The *Oberleutnant* might be a member of the Party, Bergman thought, but he's got guts and he's spoiling for a fight. And who the hell cared about politics when the enemy was in sight?

'Yes, sir. I'm with you.'

'Good. The next thing is to get a signal off to *BdU* reporting the new course and probable interception point. I think my sun fixes will be just about accurate enough. But that's a chance we'll have to take. Fortunately we don't need to surface completely but we'll have to keep an eye on that Catalina.' Bergman stopped and looked the Executive Officer straight in the eye. 'There's just one more thing. If my calculations are correct we'll be running straight into the area where the Escort Group is operating.'

'Too late to worry about that now, sir,' von Eckholdt said with a smile. 'I'm willing to die for the Fuehrer if that's what you mean.'

Well, I'm not, Bergman told himself. But I'm not going to pass up a chance to avenge Kretschmer and Schepke. Death in those circumstances at least had some point to it.

SEVEN

Bathed in the dim red glow of the night lamps the control room of *UB-44* resembled a grotesque scene from Dante's inferno. And despite the already low level of illumination inside the U-boat Bergman, von Eckholdt, and the lookouts also had their eyes shielded behind darkened goggles to give them optimum night vision as soon as they climbed out on to the bridge. Experience had taught the U-boat crews that a man's eyes normally took twenty minutes to adjust from bright light to darkness. And to ensure maximum visual efficiency it had become standard practice to light the control room with low-powered red bulbs so that the transition into darkness was less abrupt. The ex-Afrika Korps sand goggles were Bergman's own idea - and they had proved their worth on more than one occasion.

Glowing like phosphorescent ghosts, the green warning lights on the diving panel added an eerie touch of colour and the growing tension of the crew was reflected in their taut expressions as they sat at the controls waiting orders. Bergman looked up at the chronometer. It was just thirty minutes to midnight - thirty minutes to discover whether he was on the brink of the most glorious victory of his career or, he thought wryly, thirty minutes in which to discover he had made a complete ass of himself. He squared his shoulders. 'Up periscope.'

Pushing the goggles up to his forehead Bergman peered through the eyepiece. The sea was desolate and empty. His heart sank as he swung the lens full circle to search the horizon through 360°. Nothing! But it was too late to back out now. He pulled the goggles down over his eyes again.

'Down periscope. Stand by to surface.'

'Close main vents. Planes hard a-rise. Blow all tanks.' *UB-44's* skipper climbed the familiar rungs of the steel ladder as the air screamed through the pipes. Reaching up he slid the clips of the lower hatch.

'Ten feet, sir.'

The hatch cover pushed back and the sea water in the scuppers of the lower conning-tower compartment spilled over the lip into the control room. Bergman hauled himself up and started on the ladder to the upper hatch. The dog catches slipped smoothly aside and a rush of foul-smelling air funneled past him as he climbed through the circular opening on to the bridge.

The sea was calm but a layer of strata at 1,000 feet gave 10/10ths cloud cover, and not a single star was visible through the grey cotton-wool barrier protecting the sky. Bergman swore. Bang goes the chance of a quick star fix to confirm our position, he thought. Nothing seemed to be going right on this bloody patrol. He lifted the water-tight cover of the voice pipe.

'Obey bridge. Stop motors. Full ahead main engines.'

He peered down at the standard compass. 'Steer eight points to port.' The submarine's bows swung obediently in response to the rudder and, as the needle of the compass steadied along the fore-and-aft line, he said quietly, 'Helm 'midships - course now zero zero. Check and adjust gyro.'

UB-44 was now running due north at maximum speed like a ghostly grey Valkerie riding for Valhalla. But there was no matching hint of Wagnerian excitement in the heavy atmosphere. A quiet calm had descended over the bridge and, staring at the empty horizon, each man asked himself the same question - had the skipper made a mistake this time?

For Bergman there was the added bitterness of knowing that Herzog had got away with it again. There was no doubt in his mind that if the operation ended in failure the blame rested squarely on the shoulders of the coxswain, even though he had no definite proof. Bergman had sense enough to realize that any further accusations without evidence would only result in Walther sending him to face a medical board. And he could guess their verdict - unfit for combat duties and sea command. Perhaps Walther had been right. Perhaps it wasn't Herzog but 'tin disease'...

'Objects three miles on starboard quarter.'

'Stop engines!'

Bergman raised his binoculars and stared into the darkness. Three miles was the limit of visibility and the mists rising from the sea were reducing the distance every minute. He picked up a black object moving slowly against the fainter darkness behind. Then another. And another! He'd been right after all. Five minutes to midnight and the convoy was in sight. His heart jumped jubilantly. It was steaming east.

'Well done, Schoen,' he commended the lookout. 'I'll buy you a drink when we get back.' He leaned over the voice- pipe. 'Enemy in sight - stand by torpedo tubes. Full ahead both.'

UB-44's exhausts snorted exuberantly and Bergman felt the stern tuck down into the sea as the U-boat drove forward on full power. Glancing round the bridge he saw the wide grins on the faces of the men. The nagging tension had gone. Now all they wanted was action.

'We're attacking on the surface, Number One. Stand by the voice-pipe and relay steering orders. I'll co-ordinate the attack.'

The breeze had died at dusk and the mist was thickening slowly into a light fog. Ideal conditions for a surface strike at a convoy - just sufficient visibility to spot targets but thick enough to screen the U-boat from the escorts. Let's hope they haven't got radar, Bergman thought to himself. Not even fog could offer protection from the probing beams of the radar scanner.

He settled down behind the screen of the conning-tower attack station. To his right was the range-finder, on his left the telephone link to the torpedo compartment and the attack table in the control room; straight ahead was the graticuled tube of the attack sight. Thanks to recent technical improvements it was no longer necessary to aim the fore-and-aft line of the U-boat at the target. In common with her sister-boats *UB-44*'s torpedoes could now automatically take up a pre-set course within 90° of the direction in which they were fired. And that made his task a lot easier.

Sitting at the attack table in the control room, the

torpedo officer, Riedel, connected the circuits linking the bridge attack-sight with the gyro compass and waited to feed his electronic box-of-tricks with the skipper's initial settings. Once this original data had been fed into the machine it automatically digested all further course changes and passed the necessary adjustments directly to the torpedoes so that, at any given moment, they were precisely lined on the target and ready for instant firing.

Bergman lifted the telephone as he aimed the sight on the first ship. 'Lined up,' he reported.

Riedel watched the tell-tale lights on the control panel and, as they cut out, he read off the settings and passed them to Pedersen in the bow torpedo compartment.

'Bow torpedo room - settings checked, sir.'

'Follow.'

Bergman nodded as Riedel reported the intricate calculator keyed into the firing system and he held the attack- sight in his right hand to keep the cross-wires on target. Behind him von Eckholdt crouched over the voice-pipe while the lookouts kept a sharp watch for the high bow wave of a fast-moving escort. The first target loomed closer - a fat well-loaded tanker carrying enough fuel for one of the RAF's devastating 1,000-bomber raids on Berlin.

'Half speed.'

UB-44 slowed slightly and Bergman searched for the gap that would act as his gateway into the heart of the convoy. About 70° to starboard. Range closing now - three thousand yards. And, lying low on the surface, screened by the thickening fog, the pencil-slim silhouette of the U-boat remained unnoticed by the men in the convoy as they struggled to keep station in the murky darkness.

Two thousand yards. Bergman's unruffled calm gave way to a glow of exuberance as the moment of decision approached. As always his self-doubting fears evaporated in the excitement of attack and he now had no thought in his mind except the challenge ahead - although he allowed himself a moment's respite to wonder when his two comrades would show up. He glanced at his watch. One minute past midnight. No need to wait any longer.

'Fire Bow One!'

The *Type G-ye* leapt from its tube, swung on to its corrected course, and sped towards the tanker at a steady 40 knots.

'Hard right rudder!'

The U-boat twisted sharply to starboard.

'Full ahead both!'

UB-44 catapulted forward with white foam bubbling in her wake while Bergman swung the attack-sight in search of his next target. The bows of a large motor-ship suddenly appeared out of a fog bank on the starboard side but they had a good two thousand yards clearance and Bergman threw *UB-44* through the gap as he picked up a two funneled steamer in the second line. Her high sides, serried rows of lifeboats, and windowed promenade deck, identified her as a liner and he had little doubt she had been converted into a troop-carrier. The attack-sight narrowed on her beam just abaft the first funnel and he peered into the fog to estimate the range.

'Steer two points to port.'

Almost simultaneously, their initial target took *UB-44*'s first torpedo full in her belly and she erupted into a volcanic pyre of rolling flames and black oil smoke. Away in the distance, somewhere to starboard, Bergman heard the hiccup yelps of a destroyer's siren sounding the alarm.

He grinned and concentrated on the troopship. The tanker was well astern and if the escorts followed their usual pattern they would fan out south of the convoy to hunt for its attacker. And UB-44, steering for the centre of the group, was safely out of harm's way.

'Fire Bow Two!'

The second torpedo shot from its tube. A fraction of a second later Bergman altered course towards the rear of the convoy after cutting behind the troopship and doubling back along the starboard side of the second line of plodding ships. He was a good two thousand yards away when a dull thud and a sheet of flame signaled a direct hit on his second victim.

'Pedersen! Re-set running depth to seven metres.'

Bergman didn't want direct hits. They drew attention to his victim and helped to pinpoint UB-44's direction and position. What was the point of having magnetic pistols to trigger the warheads if he didn't exploit them? U-boat torpedoes were now capable of detonating as they passed beneath the keel of their victims and the resulting explosion smashed a hole in the bottom of the enemy ship, broke its back, and sent it to the bottom within minutes. And, as Bergman knew, more often than not there was no telltale flash of flame to warn the rest of the convoy. Less spectacular perhaps - but a damn sight safer.

'Running depth re-set, sir. Torpedo room standing by.'

'Hard left rudder!'

UB-44 veered through the fog towards the third line of lumbering, defenceless freighters. A shape loomed out of the darkness.

'Fire Bow Three!'

'Target aft, sir!'

Bergman's eyes whipped astern in response to

Schoen's shouted warning. The convoy was changing course, and the second line, which he had successfully bisected after firing at the troopship, was now a bare two thousand yards away. Another tanker was in direct line with the after torpedo tube. It was too good a chance to miss.

'Stern tube - fire!'

The convoy's discipline broke in panic as Bergman's third victim shuddered to a halt and began sinking by the head. The master of the vessel following immediately behind steered sharply to starboard to avert a collision while the next in line ported her helm and went full astern.

In the confusion, the torpedo from *UB-44's* stern tube missed the tanker by a hairsbreadth, streaked past its bows, and struck a small tramp steamer one thousand yards to the rear in the outer line. Suddenly ships were everywhere — ahead, astern, and on either beam. Some were turning to starboard, some to port. Others reversed course - while an enterprising Greek captain switched on all his lights and was frantically driving his boat round and round in circles with the siren blaring. It was like a busy ant's nest scattering beneath an elephant's foot.

UB-44 twisted and jinked to avoid the weaving ships and Bergman relayed a steady stream of steering orders back to von Eckholdt as he threaded the U-boat through the demoralized convoy. A star-shell rose high into the air on the port wing as an escorting corvette strove to see what was going on. But the low-lying fog swallowed the glaring brilliance of the magnesium flare with mocking ease. An ear- splitting concussion rent the air as an ammunition ship went up in a sheet of white flame and Bergman glanced back at von Eckholdt with a broad grin.

'That'll confuse the bastards. We seem to have got company. I wonder where the third boat is?'

Dismissing the question from his mind he peered ahead through the fog searching to find a suitable target for his last torpedo. A small freighter loomed into view but she failed to measure up to his ambitions.

'Two points starboard.'

UB-44 ducked away into the mists, grazed past a large tanker that had suddenly appeared from nowhere, and nosed her bows into the next fog bank. Somewhere to the right Bergman could hear the shrill yelps of a destroyer's siren as the escort commander strove to bring his scattered flock under control

Thump! Another ship erupted in flames somewhere in the distance but the fog prevented a clear view of what had happened - only the red glare reflecting through the silver- grey mist showed that one more victim was on fire. *Thump!* From the rear of the convoy this time. The third U-boat must have entered the fray. Christ! it was sheer cold-blooded murder. A massacre of the innocents.

Two more merchant ships shuddered to a halt as the magnetic torpedoes ripped gaping holes in their bottoms and Bergman could hear the shouts of the men struggling to launch the lifeboats. Hunched behind the attack-sight on *UB-44's* bridge he listened for the destroyer. The siren was louder now and she was moving fast from left to right. Suddenly the sharp grey bows of an old *V-class* veteran emerged from a fog bank. There was no time to think. Bergman centred the sight on her rust streaked hull and jabbed the firing button.

'Fire Bow Four!'

The electric torpedo left no wake and it was impossible to follow its track but *UB-44's* skipper could almost see it streaking towards the fast-moving destroyer. A fountain of dirty water rose mast-high as the warhead punched into the frail steel plates abeam the forward boiler room. There was the sharp crack of an explosion, and HMS *Weazel* circled to starboard with a heavy list and steam escaping from its ruptured boilers. She was sinking fast but, determined to sell herself dear and avenge her mortal wound, the searchlight abaft the fore funnel stabbed the darkness as it swept the surface in search of the U-boat.

'All hands clear the bridge - dive! dive! dive!'

Bergman pressed the alarm as he shouted. Almost immediately the diesels died away, the electric motors shivered to life, and he could hear the clang of the main vents opening. He followed von Eckholdt into the hatch and slammed it shut. The Executive Officer and the two lookouts tumbled down into the red glow of the control room as the skipper's feet descended through the lower hatch. The flooding valves were already wide open, the hydroplanes angled down, and *UB-44* was diving as she had never dived before.

'Lower hatch closed.'

'Twenty feet and diving, sir.'

'Take her to one hundred cox'n.' Bergman grabbed the telephone to the torpedo compartments. 'Pedersen - reload all tubes. Let's see if we can break the record. There's plenty more targets left providing Kirchen and Nachtigal don't grab them all first. And tell your lads they did a good job - everyone a winner.'

He slumped into his canvas chair and took a deep breath. As he relaxed he could hear the ominous thunderclaps of further torpedo hits and he knew the other two boats were keeping up the good work. Bergman's mouth curved sardonically. He doubted whether the shivering, oil-soaked men struggling for their lives in the cold black water thought of it in the same light. And who was to say whether he was right and they were wrong? There'd been nothing good about tonight. Just a mindless massacre of brave men without the means of defending themselves. And now he was reloading *UB-44*'s tubes ready to add to their misery. Passing his hand wearily across his face Bergman stood up and walked to the radio office.

'What did you get?' he asked Drache.

It was the wireless operator's job to pick up distress calls and identify the victims. Otherwise, unless Intelligence could confirm successes, there was no proof of the tonnage sunk. And no credit given to the captain.

'It was a bit of a job keeping up, sir,' Drache grinned.

Shut up inside his tiny office, surrounded by his transmitters and equipment, he knew nothing of the harsh realities of U-boat warfare. Cosseted and cosy he was never on the bridge to see the devastation and hear the screams - or watch the bloated oil-grimed bodies floating past in the wake of the explosion. To him it was little more than a game. Bergman did not disillusion him. The fewer who knew the truth the better. Drache handed him a sheet of paper with four names - *UB-44*'s fifth victim had gone down too fast to get off a distress call. Bergman glanced down the list and then slipped it into his pocket. Time to check them off later. Right now there was still the rest of the convoy to deal with.

Back in the control room he lifted the telephone and spoke to Pedersen.

'Loaded up yet?'

'Almost, sir. Give me three more minutes.'

Bergman could picture the sweating men in the forward torpedo compartment lifting, pushing, and swearing as they struggled to get their clumsy 3,545 lb charges into the narrow tubes. It was hard and heavy work at any time. But submerged, in action, and against the clock, it was sheer bloody torture.

'HE moving north-east, sir.'

Bergman leaned over Schiller's shoulder. 'Sure?' he demanded anxiously.

Schiller nodded. 'There are a few single ships on various bearings but the main body is proceeding north-east - speed nine knots.'

He knew he could trust his hydroplane operator. In fact he could remember that chilling moment during the *Koenig* mission when Schiller's expert ears had nearly wrecked the entire operation. He straightened up and glanced at the gyro repeater.

'Steer 2-9-0. Full ahead.'

'2-9-0, sir.'

'Group up - full ahead both.'

The telephone hanging down beside the periscope tinkled. He held it to his ear. It was Pedersen.

'Tubes re-loaded, sir. All secured.'

'Good man. Flood up.' Bergman put the telephone back on its hook. 'Stand by to surface.'

The U-boat lifted towards the surface and Bergman climbed the ladder ready to open the lower hatch. Now that the heady excitement of action was fading, the inevitable reaction was setting in. With nerves relaxed and tensions eased there was time to think. And, in the retrospect of memory, the merciless massacre he had insti-gated filled him with a loathing disgust. Clinging to the ladder with trembling hands he felt exhausted and sick.

'Ten feet, sir.'

He thrust the hatch cover up with an unthinking

reflex action and forced himself to climb on to the bridge. For the sake of his sanity the killing had to stop. He needed time to rest and wash the horrors from his mind. After this patrol he must ask Walther for a long spell of leave to give him the opportunity to purge his blood, refresh his body, and come to terms with his conscience.

Gripping the conning-tower rail Bergman knew that he must force himself to complete his task and do his duty. Yet the mere thought of another attack filled him with dread. And, as he tried to pull himself together, strangely unfamiliar temptations began floating through his mind. Perhaps, while *UB-44* submerged to reload her tubes, the convoy had disappeared. It would need no great skill to lose it. Five degrees in the wrong direction and it would be lost and gone for ever. And no one could blame him.

He stared out hopelessly into the fog praying that he would be spared a repetition of the night's horrors. The fog had thickened and visibility had fallen to three thousand yards. Nothing was in sight, and thankfully, it seemed his prayers had been answered. But for the sake of appearance he had to go through the motions. Lifting the bridge telephone he spoke to Schiller.

'Any hydrophone effect?'

'No, sir. The enemy is out of listening range.'

'Continue sweeping on a northerly bearing,' he instructed. 'I've got a hunch they'll alter course westwards to try and shake us off.'

Like hell I've got a hunch, thought Bergman. The convoy commodore must have realized he had run straight into a trap. He'll probably hold that NE course until dawn and he won't dare to double back eastwards until he's got air cover. If we keep heading north, the chances of a further enemy contact should be zero. His mouth turned down at the corners. Anyone can make a mistake he assured himself cynically. Bending over the voice-pipe he prepared to give the helmsman a fresh course that would steer them well clear of any likely trouble. But a shout from von Eckholdt made him straighten up urgently.

'Can you see that red glow, sir? Over there - fine on the port bow. If it's not the convoy it must be a damaged straggler that hasn't sunk.'

Bergman shivered as he stared into the fog bank. The Executive Officer was right, damn his eyes. He returned to the voicepipe.

'Steer two points to port - full ahead both. Stand by for action stations.'

Suddenly Bergman realized he could not stop shivering and he had to grasp the lip of the conning-tower to steady himself as he joined von Eckholdt. The red glow came closer. It was a ship - lying low in the water and ablaze from stem to stern. His stomach churned with nausea at the thought of more senseless killing. Why the hell couldn't von Eckholdt understand that enough was enough? A sour taste of bile rose in Bergman's mouth as his stomach heaved and he knew he was going to vomit. Fighting back the outward symptoms of his mental exhaustion he swung away from the rails and walked towards the open hatch.

'I'm going below, Number One. Take over I'll leave this one to you.'

He started down the ladder ashamed with himself for his weakness, yet relieved that, for once in his career, he had shrugged off the responsibilities of command. He simply must report sick when he got back to Lorient. And, until then, von Eckholdt could run *TJB-44*. All Bergman wanted now was a deep uninterrupted peaceful sleep.

Herzog looked at him curiously as he dropped down into the dim red-lit cavern of the control room, but no one spoke. The sight of the skipper's drawn grey face, sapped of vitality by lack of sleep and red-eyed with nervous strain, told them the whole story at a glance. And realizing that Bergman was on the point of collapse, Brunner stepped forward to support him in his brawny arms. Then, guiding him through the circular opening in No 4 bulkhead, he thrust the wardroom curtains aside, and helped him up on to the top bunk so that Maas was not disturbed. The skipper's body was a deadweight and Brunner found himself sweating by the time he had finished. Brushing the perspiration from his face the steward looked down. The Old Man was already fast asleep.

Someone was starting a motor-bike up on deck. Bergman opened his eyes and listened. Normally any unusual noise had him out of bed in an instant, wide awake and ready for action. But the mental and physical strain of continuous combat patrols had taken its toll and he lay on the bunk, eyes half-closed, trying to rationalize the sounds. A rasp of ripping calico tore the night air. And this time it was followed by a scream.

Machine-gun fire! Bergman's fatigue fell away instantaneously as he identified the sound that had woken him. His feet swung out of the bunk and he dropped to the floor. The men on duty in the control room looked around, startled, as he appeared through the circular hatch.

'What's going on?' he demanded.

It was the Coxswain who answered. 'The Exec

Officer is on the bridge with a machine-gun, sir. He's apparently found a boatload of enemy survivors.' That should bring the smile back to your face, Herzog thought. You and von Eckholdt are a good pair well-matched. Cold-blooded Nazi murderers. He was momentarily surprised to read the anger in the skipper's eyes.

Bergman turned away and hurried up the ladder on to the bridge to see for himself. Reaching the rails he stared out over the side. A rust-streaked lifeboat bobbed forlornly in the mid-Atlantic swell a few yards away on *UB-44*'s starboard beam. Its metal skin was ripped and torn by bullet scars and dying men hung limply over the gunwhales like tattered rag dolls. Other bodies, supported by canvas- covered life-jackets, floated face down in the water and the cold grey sea was tinted red with blood.

Bergman stood petrified with horror as he stared at the carnage. Even in a nightmare it was a scene that defied belief. And as he watched, he saw one of the seamen clamber to his feet in the stern of the lifeboat clasping a white cloth. Von Eckhodt raised the 9mm Schmeisser automatic to his shoulder, squinted through the sight, and pumped another stream of bullets at the helpless boat. The harsh hammering of the machine-gun shocked Bergman back to reality and he swung away from the rails angrily.

'Stop firing!'

The Executive Officer ignored the command and Bergman added sharply, 'That's an order!'

The man standing in the sternsheets of the lifeboat dropped the white cloth and tried to dive overboard to escape the murderous hail of fire. But a second burst smashed into his back as he stood poised ready to jump and he jerked forward into the water with a heavy splash.

Bergman could restrain himself no longer. Throwing himself across the bridge he knocked the machine-gun from the Executive Officer's hands and hurled von Eckholdt against the rail. Not realizing who was attacking him the *Oberleutnant* swung round to retaliate. But Bergman, his wrath aroused by the atrocity he had been forced to witness, gave him no time to hit back. His right arm snapped forward and his fist took von Eckholdt full on the point of his chin with every ounce of his strength behind the punch. No man could stand up to such a blow and, with a half groan, the *Oberleutnant* slumped to the floor of the bridge unconscious. But Bergman was not finished with him. His hands found von Eckholdt's throat and his clawed fingers squeezed into the soft flesh. The Executive Officer tried to fight him off but Bergman had the strength of a madman. Suddenly he felt himself being dragged away from his victim, strong arms pinioned him from behind, and a familiar voice growled in his ear.

'Easy, sir. Take it easy.'

Bergman felt the strength drain from his body as his anger evaporated and, as if someone had pulled a switch, the exhaustion crept back into his limbs. Herzog released him from the bear hug.

'I wanted to do the same, sir. But that would have been mutiny.'

The *Kapitanleutnant* did not reply. The heat of anger had passed. He was not sorry he had struck von Eckholdt. Yet, at the same time, he was ashamed that for once in his life his iron discipline had broken down to reveal his naked emotions.

'Is anyone left alive in the boat?' he asked.

'No, sir.'

Bergman took a grip on himself. He had broken the

most sacrosanct of naval regulations in full view of his crew, by striking a subordinate. And, in particular, his lapse had been witnessed by Herzog. God knew what use he would make of such a damning exhibition. Yet, for some strange reason, despite all that had happened the Coxswain's reaction seemed to be one of approval.

'*Oberleutnant* von Eckholdt is to be placed under close arrest. Take him to the wardroom and tell Essen to put him under guard.'

Standing with his arms braced on the conning-tower rail Bergman stared down at the cold, black sea as if trying to wash the horrors of the last ten minutes from his mind while the Executive Officer was taken below. He carefully avoided looking at the pathetic remains of the mutilated men in the lifeboat but he knew they were there. Von... (Eckholdt may have pulled the trigger but, as commander *op UB-44*, it was his responsibility. And if it came to the crunch he would be charged jointly with his First Officer with 'crimes against humanity'. Whatever happened it was impossible to win. If the Allies were victorious he would stand trial as a war criminal. And if Germany won he always stood in danger of facing a similar charge for sinking the *Koenig*.

'What orders, sir?' Herzog asked quietly.

Bergman pulled himself together with an effort. The needling instinct for survival spurred more deeply than ever. His personal conscience was clear whatever the evidence might suggest. And he intended to clear his name no matter what the cost. He looked around the bridge like a man who had awakened from a nightmare, only to discover that there were still four more hours to go until dawn.

UB-44 was moving north-west at half speed and the

fog was lifting. The convoy was nowhere in sight and there seemed little point in searching for it again. His crew were exhausted and he himself was in no condition to launch a further attack. What he needed now was time to sort things out.

'Alter course to the south, Coxswain. We'll dive as soon as it gets light.'

'Steer 1- 8-o!'

'1-8-o.'

'What do you intend to do about the Executive Officer, sir?' Herzog asked suddenly as he turned away from the voicepipe.

'I'm not sure,' Bergman parried. It was a question he had been churning over in his mind ever since he had ordered von Eckholdt's arrest. 'Why?'

Herzog hesitated. He moved closer to the skipper and lowered his voice confidentially. 'I reckon there's been too many mistakes made already, sir.' He paused with embarrassment. 'You know what I mean?'

Bergman had no intention of giving anything away. The sabotaged gyro was still fresh in his mind and he had not forgotten the earlier attempt on his life when he had been abandoned on the bridge of the diving U-boat. The last person he would dare to trust on board *UB-44* was the veteran Coxswain.

'I'm afraid I don't know, Cox'n. Like what?'

Herzog shied away at the challenge. 'It doesn't matter, sir. But I think you ought to know that the *Oberleutnant* is not everything he's supposed to be.'

'How do you mean?'

'I mean he's not a *Kriegsmarine* U-boat officer, sir. If I were you I'd be a bit careful over this arrest business.'

Bergman hoped that the shadows hid the shock in his

face. Herzog had a reputation for obtaining information from the most unlikely sources - his long years of service in the U- boat branch had brought him contacts that many senior officers would have envied. He was puzzled by the Coxswain's sudden and unexpectedly friendly attitude. He chose his words carefully and maintained his guard.

'I agree that *Oberleutnant* von Eckholdt was rather stale on his routines when he joined us. But, of course, he'd been attached for Special Duties for some time. Until today he had been a first-class officer in every way.'

Herzog puffed himself up with self-importance as he delivered his bombshell.

'Did you know that he has been sending unauthorized radio messages back to Lorient, sir?'

Bergman felt an ice-cold finger of fear slide down his back. What was Herzog trying to do - bluff him into some sort of confession. Or did he now face the possibility of having two traitors in his crew.

'What evidence do you have?' he demanded.

'*Funkobermaat* Drache told me, sir. He sent the messages for the *Oberleutnant*. He understood you had given permission.'

Bergman turned towards the hatch. 'We'll soon sort this out, Cox'n. The signals will be logged and recorded. I intend to hear what Drache has to say about the matter.'

Herzog reached out to hold him back. 'It won't do any good, sir,' he explained. 'They were supposed to be private messages to a girlfriend or something. Drache didn't log them because he knew it was forbidden to transmit unofficial signals. But there's something else you ought to know. Both of the messages were in code. And it wasn't one of the official Navy cyphers.'

For once in his life Bergman was frightened. If Herzog were telling the truth, *UB-44* could be in imminent danger - there was no knowing what lay behind von Eckholdt's mysterious signals. And if *BdU's* receivers had intercepted the messages, harmless or not, he was going to be called upon to do a great deal of explaining when he arrived back in Lorient The dilemma deepened even on casual reflection. Obviously Drache would back up Herzog's story. Yet how could he know if they were telling the truth. It might all be part of one gigantic trick skillfully engineered by the Coxswain to land him in further trouble.

Surprisingly, there was one point about which he felt quite confident. He didn't like von Eckholdt but his loyalty to the Fuehrer was so fanatically intense that Bergman could not imagine him turning traitor. If he was not a traitor, and if the stories of the secret signals were correct, it could mean only one thing. The Executive Officer had been deliberately planted in *UB-44* as a spy, probably by the Gestapo. And the only person on board the U-boat likely to be under suspicion was himself.

Bergman felt a cold bead of perspiration trickle down his back as he digested the theory and his brain spun wildly as he tried to make sense of the unexpected situation now confronting him. He flipped back the cover of the voicepipe to the control room.

'Riedel! I want you topsides. Take over the watch.' He turned to Herzog. 'Thank you for telling me, Chief. I'll keep the matter confidential. There's probably nothing in it. Keep an eye on young Reidel when he takes over the watch - he's still a bit green. I'll be in the wardroom if I'm wanted.' Bergman waited until the Second Officer was safely on the bridge and his eyes had adjusted for efficient night vision. Then after a brief reminder to dive at dawn, he slipped down the conning-tower ladder.

Von Eckholdt looked up as the skipper pushed aside the curtains and entered the wardroom. Maas had returned to his quarters in the forward crew space the previous evening and the two men were alone in the tiny airless compartment. There was a livid bruise on the *Oberleutnant's* chin but, otherwise, he seemed none the worse for his experience and there was no resentment in his eyes as he waited. Bergman had already decided what he intended to do and he wasted no time on preambles.

'I'm sorry I lost my temper, Number One.'

The Executive Officer ignored the apology and concentrated on the hard facts of the situation. 'Am I still under arrest?' he asked coldly.

Bergman sat down opposite von Eckholdt and faced him levelly across the width of the narrow wardroom table. The *Oberleutnant* watched him warily.

'I will answer that question in a few moments,' Bergman told him, 'but right now there are more important things to discuss. I'll be perfectly honest with you. I can't afford to run this boat with the help of only one inexperienced Watch Officer. But, at the same time, it is impossible for me to overlook what happened earlier and it remains my duty to hand you over on a court martial charge when we return to base. In the meantime I will propose a compromise. If you will agree to carry out your normal Watch Officer duties I am prepared to cancel my orders for your arrest.' He paused for a moment and then continued, 'I must remind you that you will remain at full liberty to report me under the Navy Discipline Regulations for striking you.'

Von Eckholdt gave no indication of what was going on

in his mind. He stood up, clicked his heels, and bowed stiffly. 'I appreciate your candour, *Herr Kapitanleutnant.* For once we are in agreement. Whatever our personal differences might be, the safety of *UB-44* must take priority.' He, too, paused. And the hesitation was carefully timed to add impact to his next statement. 'You must do *your* duty, sir. You will understand that *I* must do mine also.'

Bergman's eyes narrowed thoughtfully as the *Oberleutnant* pushed through the curtains and returned to the control room. Well, you bastard, he thought to himself. I've given you the rope. Now which of us is going to hang? You - or me?

EIGHT

The Gestapo knocked on the door of 17 Rue de Ville at 4-02 a.m. precisely. The hour before dawn, when resistance and morale was at its lowest ebb, was their favourite visiting time. Standing on the edge of the pavement *Gruppenfuehrer* Gorst stared up at the curtained windows searching for a sign of movement. He nodded impatiently and Dorfmann repeated his tattoo on the wrought-iron knocker. There was an echo of footsteps inside the house, a creaking of bolts being slid, and the door swung open to reveal the frightened face of the concierge. Dorfmann and his two companions pushed past her into the dingy entrance hall and fanned out ready to shoot anyone trying to escape through the back of the house. Gorst snapped his fingers imperiously.

'Resident's Register.'

Madame Roche pulled a battered blue covered book from the drawer of an equally ancient bureau standing by the stairs and handed it over. Gorst blew off the dust and flicked the pages with his thumb to find the latest entries. He glanced down the list quickly.

'First floor - room six,' he told Dorfmann.

Rahel was already dressed and waiting as they burst through the door of her room. Three years on the run, first in Germany and then in France, had made her familiar with the dawn visit. And the instinct of the hunted warned her that this time the Gestapo had come for her. Even if they hadn't, it was essential that they did not search the house further.

'Your papers, mam'selle.'

Rahel could have handed the *Gruppenfuehrer* the carefully doctored set of identity papers that Johann had obtained two years earlier for her in Kiel. Papers that gave her name as Elke Fraenkel. But with Eckstein and his printing press hidden in the attic she knew she must divert attention to herself to give him time to escape. Opening her bag she drew out the other set of false papers which had been specially prepared to meet such a situation as this. They were blatant forgeries intended to deceive no one. But she gave no hint of the fear in her heart as she handed them over to the Gestapo officer.

Gorst stared down at them and almost sneered at the clumsily executed fake. She must have been a complete fool to imagine he would be deceived so easily.

'You are Fraulein Rahel Yousoff?' There was the faintest of question marks at the end of the statement as if Gorst knew that he was merely reciting a proven fact.

She stared back at him coolly. So they had come for her. Eckstein should be quite safe in his hiding place if she did nothing to arouse their suspicions. She nodded.

'Yes - I am Rahel Yousoff.'

The *Gruppenfuehrer* glanced at her sharply but Rahel's expressionless eyes met his without flinching. He stuffed the identity papers into the pocket of his black raincoat.

'Come with us, please.' Gorst was always polite. He found no need to be rude. People never argued with the Gestapo.

Sitting in the back seat of the Mercedes as they drove back to Gestapo Headquarters in the Avenue Foche, Rahel prayed that she would have the strength to keep her secrets safely locked in silence. The German resistance movement was growing in strength every week but, compared with its counterparts in the occupied countries, it was a puny ineffective organization capable of little more than anti-Nazi propaganda. Even the British would not take them seriously and without support from London they were isolated and powerless to act decisively.

And so, a few months previously, she had travelled into France on a false pass as a representative of the ZFF - the Zionist Freedom Front - in an attempt to contact the French Resistance movement, in the hope that the two organizations could co-operate and unify their efforts against the common enemy. So far she had been unsuccessful. The French had been naturally suspicious of a German probing into their secrets, and every attempt she made to contact the Resistance leaders had been carefully blocked. No one, it seemed, would take her seriously. And those who did kept their mouths closed in fear. The retribution of the Maquis could be just as swift and brutal as that of the enemy.

On her arrival at Gestapo headquarters Rahel was taken to a reception office for preliminary examination - a routine form-filling exercise by a quiet bespectacled clerk who noted down a summary of her personal history that delved back as far as her grandparents' origins and ages.

Any facts that could be checked easily against official records were answered truthfully but Rahel was well prepared for her arrest and she carefully inserted a number of half-truths and downright lies to make the checking more difficult and time consuming. And she was careful to maintain her cover - that she was a teacher who had come to Paris in search of work because her racial background was unacceptable in Germany.

The second interrogation proved to be more searching but Rahel felt that she had maintained her story successfully. She was relieved to discover that the rumours of Gestapo brutality she had heard repeated so many times in the past five years seemed without foundation. The questioning had been intensive and tough but her interrogators had treated her with polite correctness throughout the long, three-hour session. And never once had anyone offered even the slightest threat of physical violence.

Her feelings of relief proved to be short-lived. When she found herself facing *Gruppenfuehrer* Gorst in the notorious Room 15, she sensed that the gloves were off. Yet, unexpectedly, even he treated her gently and it was only after two further hours of intensive grilling that she began to realize that the Gestapo were not interested in her current liaison activities with the French underground - they were working much closer to home. The connection between Group Anton, her old Communist cell in Kiel, and the *Kriegsmarine*. And, more especially, the U-boat service.

Rahel went suddenly quiet as Gorst switched his line of interrogation. She had broken her links with Group Anton early in 1940 and she had not prepared herself to parry questions into her activities so long ago. This was the end of the cat-and-mouse game. From now on she did not dare answer anything for fear of inadvertently betraying an old comrade. But not even then did she realize where Gorst's questioning was leading.

'I met your old friend *Kapitanleutnant* Bergman in Lorient a few weeks ago,' the *Gruppenfuehrer* whispered hoarsely. 'You were lovers, I believe?'

Her heart leapt violently at the mention of Konrad's name but she kept her lips closed. How did he come into all this?

'Come, come, Fraulein Yousoff. We know all about your little affair - what was wrong with it? Most girls would envy you the chance of a famous U-boat captain.' He chuckled. 'You were the *Kapitanleutnant*'s mistress?'

Rahel's stubborn silence only served to infuriate Gorst. He persevered with the same line of questioning. Hoess and Belzec were brought into assist and, an hour later, Rahel was bleeding from the mouth and livid bruises marred her pale skin. But despite the blows, she steadfastly refused to admit any knowledge of the U-boat commander.

Gorst's eyes blazed with anger. He knew Rahel held the vital key that Himmler needed, and he was prepared to do anything to gain the information. His promotion and his career depended on breaking her down, and he had no reservations concerning the methods necessary to obtain what he wanted. If the Gestapo could prove that the Navy was being infiltrated by subversive elements, the last restraints on its power would be removed. With such proof, even the *Fuehrer* would have to yield to Himmler's demands for authority over the armed forces. And once that authority were granted, it was only a short step to absolute control of the German State by the SS.

Faced by such a dazzling prize there was no room for scruples.

Rahel shivered as she saw Hoess carry the electrical apparatus into the room and place it carefully on the table. She knew what they intended to do and she prayed to the God of Abraham and Moses that he would give her the strength to resist. Belzec came behind her, thrust her down on to a wooden chair, and pulled her arms back. She closed her eyes as the leather straps bit into her wrists. Gorst leaned forward, gripped her chin in his fingers, and forced her to look up into his face.

'Just admit that *Kapitanleutnant* Bergman was your lover,' he urged hoarsely. 'I will see that all charges against you are dropped.' He played on her emotions. 'Why try to defend him? He doesn't care about you any longer. He's got some fancy French woman back in Lorient to keep his bed warm for him.'

Rahel stared back at him. 'I do not know this man you are talking about,' she said simply.

Gorst shrugged. His fingers began to unfasten the buttons of her blouse. 'In that case, fraulein, we must do something to jog your memory.'

Her body went rigid as he opened her blouse and tugged the brassiere roughly aside. His fingers were like cold moist snakes probing her flesh and Rahel shuddered with disgust as he clipped the two electrodes in place. Leaning forward across the electrical apparatus Hoess's mouth gaped expectantly as he waited Gorst's signal to begin. The *Gruppenfuehrer* nodded curtly and he began to turn the handle of the manual generator with eager obedience.

Rahel's bubbling shriek of pain woke Bergman from his sleep with a sudden start. He sat up sharply in his bunk, his skin clammy with sweat, and his brain still echoing with the woman's screams as he stared wildly around the empty wardroom. Shaking his head, he rubbed his hand across his face, and tried to throw off the ghastly nightmare that had shocked him awake. Then, lying back on the bunk, he tried to collect his thoughts and recall the details of the dream. But there was no dream to remember - only a scream. A woman's scream.

Bergman knew it was useless to try to sleep again. His nightmares had continued without respite for the last six days, and he was at the end of his tether. Perhaps when they arrived back in Lorient later today and he could feel the solid earth beneath his feet again he would be able to think straight. Pushing his legs out of the bunk he dropped to the floor and walked across to the coffee-pot. He put it on the electric ring to warm up while he paced the room trying to gather his thoughts.

The wardroom was empty. Von Eckholdt and Riedel were on watch in the control room and *UB-44* was making her final approach to Lorient submerged - the RAF's Liberator patrols over the approaches to the U-boat bases made it too dangerous to remain on the surface in French coastal waters. There was a certain irony in the situation that appealed to Bergman's sense of humour for, despite their continued ascendancy in mid-Atlantic, Doenitz's victorious sea wolves were now forced to skulk back to their concrete- roofed, bomb-proof lairs out of sight beneath the surface to escape the predators of the skies, instead of returning in triumph for the world to see.

Pouring himself a steaming mug of coffee Bergman sat down wearily at the table. For the fiftieth time in as many hours he ran over the events of the past few weeks in an effort to rationalize his fears. But the tangled web of intrigue and suspicion only become more involved each time he reviewed the facts, and he felt his sanity reeling as he tried to make sense of all that happened.

He had questioned the radio operators and confirmed Herzog's story that von Eckholdt had sent two signals back to Lorient even though there was no entry in the signal log and no record of the messages. Both men had insisted that the signals had been transmitted in a code they could not identify.

Of course the whole incident could be part of an elaborate plot by Herzog to plant the seeds of doubt and suspicion in his mind in order to turn him against the Executive Officer and divert attention from himself. God knows, a U-boat commander's life was lonely enough without the worries of having a potential traitor on board. But perhaps that was also part of the Coxswain's plan. He must have known that his skipper was under stress and suffering from combat fatigue. Perhaps he had concocted the story in order to push him over the edge.

Bergman sipped his coffee moodily. Apart from von Eckholdts's stupidity in shooting up the lifeboat he had behaved with the utmost correctness both before and after that incident. And Bergman was under no illusions that, in his present state of health, UB-44 would never have made it back from patrol without the Executive Officer's assistance.

Yet there was still something in the man's make-up that he did not trust. The fact that he was a die-hard Nazi did not help, for Bergman was rapidly coming to loathe and detest anything remotely connected with the Fuehrer and his crazy creed of racialism and oppression. But von Eckholdt seemed to harbour no resentment over the lifeboat episode and in fact, since that time, had shown a remarkable desire to help relieve him from the stresses and pressures of command. One thing, however, continued to nag at Bergman's mind. The *Oberleutnant* seemed surprisingly unworried by the threat of the court martial charge hanging over his head. And that, in Bergman's present unhappy state of mind, was discomfortingly significant.

Then there was Herzog. He still had no doubts that the Coxswain had tried to murder him and he was equally sure that he was trouble-making when he reported von Eckholdt's mysterious radio messages. Yet he, too, had shown a remarkable *volte face* since the lifeboat incident. The old antagonisms had evaporated overnight and he had reverted to his previous helpfulness that had made him the mainstay of *UB-44* in the early days of the war.

The war. Bergman shivered uncontrollably at the memory of the convoy massacre he had engineered and led earlier in the patrol. And of all the other defenceless ships he had destroyed in the course of his short but eventful career. Would it ever be possible to wash the blood from his hands? Thank God he still had Michelle. At least she was the one person in the world he could talk to and who could understand. Each time he returned from patrol he revealed more and more of his thoughts to her. Perhaps this time he should tell her everything. Perhaps it might be the only way to save his sanity before it was too late.

'Stand by to surface.'

They must be running into the rendezvous area. He could picture the minesweeper nestling in the lee of Belle lie waiting their return. The quick flash of the interrogative signal from her bridge. *UB-44's* reply. And then the brief: *Follow me*. Then the slow, relaxing miles of the last lap, with the crew lining the fore-deck casing as the salt-grimed U-boat steamed to her berth in the Commercial harbour before passing in through the vast reinforced concrete portals of the submarine pens.

'You are a sick man, *Kapitanleutnant*. You must report to the Flotilla Surgeon immediately.'

Kapitan Walther, the flotilla commander, was worried. He had seen U-boat commanders crack up under the relentless strain many times before, and he recognized the unmistakable symptoms. Bergman was almost the last of the flotilla's old 'aces' and he had endured considerably more stress than any of his contemporaries. Now it was time to call a halt.

Bergman swayed on his feet with fatigue but he stood his ground. 'I promise to report sick as soon as I leave this office, *Herr Kapitan*. But I insist you investigate my charge against *Oberleutnant* von Eckholdt. If we do not act against our own war criminals how can we expect justice from the enemy when our time comes?'

'Calm down, Bergman. A short while ago you were accusing Herzog of trying to kill you. Now you charge your Executive Officer with war crimes and tell me some cock- and-bull story about mysterious radio signals. Really, *Kapitanleutnant,* are you trying to prove you are mad?'

Somehow the tone in Walther's voice made it an unconvincing reprimand and Bergman suspected there was something more to come. The Flotilla Commander sat down and stared at the file spread out on top of his desk. He seemed to be making his mind up about something and he made a vague gesture to Bergman to take a seat.

There was a long pause before Walther made his decision. 'I propose to break one of the strictest rules of the service,' he said quietly. 'But I know you well enough to trust you. Will you give me your word that this will go no further? And that when you have heard me out you may be prepared to change your views?'

UB-44's skipper nodded. 'You have my word, *Kapitan*. But it is extremely unlikely that you can tell me anything to persuade me to drop my charges against von Eckholdt.' Walther sighed. He could see it was going to be an uphill battle. '*Oberleutnant* von Eckhold is a member of the Fuehrer's personal staff,' he explained briefly. 'He was assigned to *UB-44* on the Fuehrer's special instructions. And he has already left Lorient. He was flown back to the *Wolfsschanze[1]* an hour after you berthed.'

Bergman's astonishment showed in his face. 'But why was he assigned to *UB-44 to my* boat.'

Walther shrugged. 'I have no idea,' he replied but his disclaimer did not sound very convincing.

'So the radio signals were probably reports about me - a spy sending messages back to his masters.'

'Nothing so sinister, I'm sure, Bergman,' the Kapitan said soothingly. 'It is much more probable he was making private arrangements for the aircraft to pick him up.' Walther hesitated again. Then, leaning forward across the desk in a confidential manner, he took the plunge. 'I know I shouldn't tell you this, *Kapitanleutnant,* but having gone this far I suppose I might as well. There are rumours on the grapevine that the Fuehrer is taking a personal interest in you.'

'Me?'

It seemed ludicrous. Despite his successes Bergman knew he was probably the most disloyal U-boat commander in the entire *Kriegsmarine*. What other middle-ranking officer was actively weighing his opportunities of overthrowing and his evil regime. If Walther had not been so deadly serious he would have laughed in his face.

'Yes, Bergman, you. Doenitz has to send a resume of your latest combat report to the *Wolfsschanze* each time you return from patrol. The Staff of *BdU* are certain you are destined for great things — and I can assure you that the Fuehrer does not take an interest in particular officers without reason. So take my advice and drop this charge against von Eckholdt. It will obviously serve no purpose. And it could well harm your career.'

'And if I don't?'

Walther shrugged expressively. 'It will never be delivered. You do not imagine that I or any other senior officer on the Staff would endorse a document accusing one of the Fuehrer's personal staff with - er - an alleged crime. I have no doubt that the *Oberleutnant* had good reason for opening fire. And you have admitted yourself that you were not on the bridge at the beginning of the incident.'

Bergman was too disgusted to reply. If this was the attitude of his superior officers no wonder Germany was doomed to defeat. Let one single private soldier or ordinary seaman step out of line and he would be executed on the spot. But if the Fuehrer's favourites were involved then all eyes must be tightly closed, no matter what the crime. He stood up.

'In that case, *Herr Kapitan*,' he said icily, 'the matter is closed. With your permission I wish to be relieved of my command.'

'Permission refused,' Walther snapped curtly. 'If you were not a sick man I'd call you a damned young fool. As it is I can sympathize. I propose to put you on immediate sick leave and you are to arrange for an examination by the Flotilla Surgeon without delay. And keep away from that damned boat of yours until you are fit for duty.'

Bergman hurried down the stairs from Walther's office in a cold rage. At least he knew where he stood — and where the Navy stood. After this latest revelation he had little doubt where Germany stood either. Leaving the building by the main entrance he made his way across to the Hotel Beau Sejour where the senior combat officers were billeted when ashore. He stopped in the vestibule to collect his mail. The clerk handed him two letters which he recognized as being addressed in his mother's hand-writing and another smaller envelope, postmarked Kiel, in an unfamiliar script. Turning into the lounge to read his mail he found himself buttonholed by another officer. It was Kessel, commander of *UB-48*.

'Sorry to hear the news, Konrad,' Kessel said quietly. 'It's always sad when it's a friend as well as a flotilla mate.'

Bergman stopped and gathered his thoughts. 'What news?' he asked. 'I only berthed at noon and I've spent most of my time with Walther since then. What's happened?'

'It's Hans - Hans Kirchen. They got *UB-203* after the convoy attack. I heard about it in the War Room just after lunch. They're issuing a special communique this evening.' Bergman felt the room rotate. Kirchen was one of his oldest friends in the service. They'd been fellow cadets at the Academy before the war and had both been through the Periscope School together in 1937. He could still remember the night when they had beaten up the three SA men - the night, incidentally, that had led to his first meeting with Rahel. And now he was dead.

'How did it happen?'

'They were caught on the surface by an Escort Group. Apparently they were picking up survivors when the enemy appeared out of a fog bank. One of the destroyers rammed *UB-203* amidships and Hans was crushed against the periscope standard.'

Bergman passed a hand across his face. He could feel the wetness of tears on his cheeks and he turned away to hide his grief from Kessel. Stumbling unseeing into the hotel lounge he sat down in one of the large leather chairs in front of the fireplace.

What sort of crazy world were they living in? Hans had been killed while trying to save survivors - killed by the comrades of the men he was attempting to rescue. Yet von Eckholdt had escaped scot free after mercilessly gunning down the men in the lifeboat. What sort of a God could allow such things to happen. And what dark powers of evil did Hitler control that could protect the guilty and punish the innocent.

He suddenly recalled his recent interview with Walther. Perhaps he had been chosen to survive because he, too, was one of the guilty. But why should the Fuehrer take an interest in him? Had he become such an epitome of evil that even Hitler recognized him as an ally? Bergman probed back into his past career as he searched for answers. And he knew there could be only one reason - the *Koenig*. Obviously the Fuehrer had been so impressed by his blind, unreasoning obedience to orders — orders that had led him to murder a thousand innocent German sailors - that he was thinking of using him again on some similar mission of horror.

UB-44's skipper stared into the fire as he digested his conclusion. Perhaps, on reflection, it would be advantageous to encourage the Fuehrer's belief in his loyalty. It would at least give him an opportunity of getting closer to the dictator. And a time could well come when he could exploit such a position to rid Germany of the madman who was riding it to destruction.

So that was why von Eckholdt was spying on him. To test his loyalty to the Fuehrer. Bergman thought back over the patrol and smiled. Provided his ex-Executive Officer did not hold his bruised chin against him he had very good reasons for supposing that Hitler would shortly be reading yet another glowing commendation of his skills.

He began to slit open the Kiel envelope and he frowned down at the typewritten note inside.

Your friend has been arrested. You must disown her as she
will disown you. It is not for your sake but for Germany.
Your time will come. Until then do nothing to cause suspicion. Burn this.

There was no signature but Bergman sensed it was genuine. Crumpling the paper into a ball he threw it into the fire and watched the flames consume it. So Rahel was alive. In any other circumstances he would have felt glad at the news. But the knowledge that she was in the hands of the Gestapo only added to his present anguish. Better she were dead.

'*Kapitanleutnant* Bergman?' Konrad looked up as the waiter paged the room. He nodded.

'Excuse me, *m'sieur le Capitan,* but there is a

gentleman downstairs asking for you. He would not give his name.' Bergman knew who was waiting long before he walked down the stairs and saw the black leather raincoat and black felt hat, trade-marks of the Gestapo. So the betrayal was complete. They had traced Rahel's connection with him and were closing in for the kill. Hiding his fears under a boldly confident innocence he walked up to the squat figure of Otto Gorst.

'I am *Kapitanleutnant* Bergman.' He clicked his heels and bowed stiffly. 'You wish to see me?'

Gorst acknowledged the introduction with a beaming smile. 'An honour, my dear *Kapitanleutnant*. It is not often I meet such a famous U-boat hero.'

'What can I do for you?' Bergman asked with a hint of impatience in his voice. 'Is one of my men in trouble?'

The Gestapo officer guided him to one side. 'I wonder, *Herr Kapitanleutnant,* whether you can do me a small favour. I believe you served in Kiel before the war?'

'Yes - but it was many years ago now.'

'Quite so, quite so. It is only a matter of routine identification, you understand. You are not involved in any way. We have arrested a certain person whom we believe was obtaining information on U-boat movements. We found them in Lorient and our information leads us to think there is some link with a notorious terrorist group in North Germany. Perhaps you would be good enough to come with me to see if you might identify the prisoner.' Gorst shrugged expressively and his hoarse whisper grew a fraction more sibilant. 'I realize I am taking up your valuable time, *Herr Kapitanleutnant,* but if you can help in this matter of identification it will greatly assist our enquiries.'

So the trap had been sprung. And sooner than he had

expected. Bergman wondered why he had never considered the possibility that Rahel was already in Lorient. Obviously the Gestapo had brought her to the U-boat base so that he could produce no excuses for refusing to see her. A trip to Paris or to Kiel would have afforded him ample reasons for avoiding the confrontation. But here, on the doorstep, it was impossible. And the Gestapo was relying on the shock of unexpected recognition to give them away. Thank God he had received the note forewarning him of Rahel's arrest.

'Very well, *Herr* Gorst. I suppose I must do my duty even if it is a trifle socially inconvenient.'

He climbed into the Mercedes standing at the kerbside and settled back into the rear seat as the driver weaved it through a maze of dingy streets towards the Rue de Navarre.

This was surely the end of the road for both of them and he was by no means convinced that the anonymous letter contained good advice. As a realist he knew perfectly well that there was nothing he could do to overthrow the Nazi regime. Even looking into the future, he saw little hope of ever doing so, either personally, or as part of a team. So, in the circumstances, why not sacrifice himself if it gave Rahel a chance of freedom? He was the one they really wanted.

He followed Gorst up the narrow stairs to the office on the first floor. The *Gruppenfuehrer* locked the door carefully, checked that everything was secure and picked up the internal telephone.

'Dorfmann — bring the prisoner in.'

Bergman felt his heart hammering inside his chest as he waited but, outwardly, he remained calmly disinterested. Could he save her, or was it too late? The door to the anteroom opened and, hardened though he was to the horrors of war, Bergman could not restrain a gasp as Rahel was helped into the office.

Her clothing was dirty and torn and she hobbled painfully as if her feet were bruised. Her eyes were dull and dark circles beneath them added to her haggard appearance. She seemed like a broken doll - listless and lifeless. She looked up at him blankly for a moment and then stared down at the floor. There was no hint of recognition in her face.

'Well?' whispered Gorst.

It had been almost two years since Bergman had last seen Rahel and, even had he wanted to, it was difficult to believe that this pitiful wreck was the same woman. He shook his head.

'Never seen her in Kiel?'

'Not that I can remember, but then it would be difficult to recognize anyone after the Gestapo have had their hands on them.'

Gorst's eyes flickered momentarily but he ignored the insult. Walking across to Rahel he twisted his hands in her hair and wrenched her head up to look at Bergman.

'Is this the man you told us about?'

'No ... I've never seen him before.'

Gorst thrust her head down with a brutal jerk. He swore. So much for his schemes to get promotion. He knew they were both lying but he had no proof. He could work on the girl but he doubted if he would achieve anything. And the regulations - the very regulations he was scheming to destroy - prevented him from taking any action against Bergman. Fighting back his angry frustration, he croaked an order at Dorfmann to take her away.

Bergman waited until the door was closed and they

were alone. He felt suddenly confident. The knowledge that the Fuehrer was showing an interest in him gave him an unexpected power, and he savoured the thought of Gorst squirming. If the Gestapo officer tried to cause difficulties Bergman now had little doubt who would win the encounter. Not even Himmler would dare to strike against one of Hitler's favourites.

'Now that this distasteful charade is over, Herr Gorst, I intend to make a report of the matter. I am not unaware of the insinuations you have been making and I shall communicate direct to the Fuehrer.'

Gorst shifted his feet awkwardly. There was something unnerving about Bergman's confidence and years of combat command had given him an air of authority that demanded instant obedience.

'You have misunderstood my intentions, *Herr Kapitanleutnant,* ' he wheedled hoarsely. 'As I explained earlier it was just a routine matter of identifying a suspected person. There is no harm in that, surely?'

'What do you intend to do to the woman?'

Gorst shrugged. 'She has admitted to certain technical offences. She will probably be sent to a labour camp - Dachau or Ravensbruck - for a few months and, when she has served her sentence, she will be released.'

Bergman accepted the assurance as it was given. Like most Germans he had no knowledge of the concentration camps or Hitler's policy of mass extermination. Gorst's explanation sounded reasonable.

'There is just one more thing, *Herr Gruppenfuehrer.* I have spent most of this war at sea in U-boats and my loyalty to the Fatherland is beyond question. I cannot understand how you came to imagine I had any connection with this affair, whatever it may be.'

'We receive a great deal of information, *Herr Kapitan-leutnant*. It is not Gestapo policy to reveal its sources.' Gorst certainly had no intention of revealing Herzog's telephone call. His only chance of retrieving the situation was to hope that more information would come in and although the call had been anonymous, he had always felt sure that it had come from one of *UB-44*'s crew. If so there was always the chance that the man would supply further details.

Bergman picked up his cap and looked pointedly at the locked door. Gorst hurried to open it.

'I will be making my report this evening, *Herr Grup-penfuehrer*. I suggest that you make sure your sources of information are reliable before your superiors start asking questions. Good day.'

Gorst closed the door behind him and sat down at his desk. Bergman had escaped the carefully laid trap and his hopes of impressing Berlin with his skill had suffered a resounding blow. The woman was useless now, and she could be disposed of without difficulty. But somehow he had to obtain evidence against *UB-44*'s captain if he wanted to salvage something from the wreckage of his schemes. And, fortunately, he still had one immediate source of information even though, so far, it had failed to yield much in the way of value. Picking up the telephone *Gruppenfuhrer* Gorst asked the operator for a Lorient number.

Bergman walked away from the Gestapo office like a man in the midst of a nightmare but, aware that hidden eyes were probably following him, he resolutely forced himself not to look back at the upper windows where Rahel was being held prisoner. The shock of seeing her remained vividly in his mind and, walking slowly, he brooded on her fate.

As he turned the corner he recalled the letter he had received from Kiel that afternoon. *Your time will come. Do nothing until then.* Do nothing! That was the trouble. He had done nothing. And look where it had ended. From now on he intended to prepare himself for the challenge that lay ahead. And, when the time came, they — whoever they were - would find him ready. A system of government that could produce monsters like Gorst must be destroyed if the Fatherland was to survive. And to- *Kapitanleutnant* Bergman the survival of his beloved Germany was the only thing that mattered.

Crossing the road he realized that he was only a few hundred yards from Michelle's apartment. He was in desperate need of someone to talk to, and unconsciously he quickened his pace. Suddenly he was struck by an unexpected doubt that made him stop in the middle of the pavement. Why, for the first time since their relationship had begun, had she not been at the quayside to welcome him home. Surely...?

On an impulse Bergman turned into the cafe that stood on the corner of the block and found himself an empty table by the window. The proprietor, a veteran of Verdun, took his order with the air of a man who did not like German customers in his establishment. And, when it came, the coffee was bitter and revolting. But Bergman scarcely tasted it - his mind was too busy digesting the disturbing doubts that suddenly confronted him. Leaving the table he walked across to the counter.

'Do you have a telephone, m'sieur?' he asked politely.

The cafe proprietor jerked his thumb towards the wall. 'Over there,' he mumbled ungraciously. He went back to his magazine while Bergman dialed a Paris number and waited to be connected.

'Put me through to Kapitan Stohr,' he told the operator when she answered.

'Official or personal?'

'It's none of your damned business. Do as I ask.'

There was another interval and Bergman could imagine her sulkily delaying the connection as long as she dared. As he waited, he wondered why he hadn't thought of checking before. But he could be a damned fool when he was out of his natural element under the sea. It was lucky he remembered Stohr being transferred to the POW liaison section at Doenitz's Paris headquarters. Ludwig had been skipper of *UB-16* when he had served as the submarine's junior Watch Officer and, although they had met only infrequently since the outbreak of war, the two men had remained in touch when duties permitted.

'Hello — Kapitan Stohr speaking.'

'Konrad Bergman here, Ludwig. Listen, this is important. Can you do me a favour in a hurry?'

'Naturally, Konrad. What's the flap? You sound a bit fraught.'

'Will you check the French Navy records for a Jules Lamartine. He might be a POW or he might be dead. He was supposed to have been drowned in a French sub — *Le Plongeur* - when it went down in the early part of 1940.'

'Okay. Hang on a few minutes. I'll do a quick run through the index.'

Bergman fed another handful of coins into the box and waited. Why the hell hadn't he checked Michelle's story before? There had always been something odd about the way they had met. And their relationship itself.

Knowing the Gestapo it wasn't difficult to guess what had happened. Her husband was probably in a prison camp and Gorst was using him as a lever to force his wife to act as a spy. It would be typical of Gestapo methods. Bergman listened intently as Stohr picked up the receiver at the other end of the line.

'You there, Konrad? Good. I think you must have got your facts wrong. There's no officer or rating by the name of Lamartine on our files and I even looked up the French Navy List for March 1940 as a double check. I'm afraid he doesn't exist.'

Bergman stood there stunned but he managed to murmur his thanks to his old skipper for his assistance.

'Don't hang up yet, Konrad,' Stohr broke in. 'There's something else. There is no record of a submarine called *Le Plongeur* in the French Navy either.'

Bergman's brain was reeling as he put the phone down. So Michelle was a fraud. She wasn't the widow of a naval officer. Her name probably wasn't even Lamartine. He turned to the cafe proprietor who was still intent on his magazine. He slipped a French banknote on the counter.

'Do you know the woman who lives at Number 18 - Madame Lamartine?'

Raoul might have disliked Germans but he had a fondness for French money. He slipped the note into the capacious pocket of his white apron.

"You mean the blonde? The one with the big...'

Bergman nodded. 'Yes - that's her. Tell me, how long has she been living in Lorient?'

Raoul thought for a moment. 'Not that long,' he said slowly. 'Must have come here soon after the surrender.' He paused. 'Yes, that's about it. Some time in June 1940.

She said something about coming from Alsace to avoid the bombing.'

Bergman left the cafe and walked slowly to the door of Apartment 18. So that was it. Michelle had arrived at the beginning of the Occupation. And she came from an area of France with a history of German connections. Her French would naturally be fluent - but her parents were almost certainly of German origin. Gorst must have planted her in Lorient to act as a Gestapo spy.

She looked surprised when she saw Bergman standing at the door. But she recovered quickly and invited him into the luxuriously furnished lounge where they had spent so many evenings in the past.

'This is a pleasant surprise, cheri,' she told him. 'I didn't realize you were back. I would have been down to the harbour as usual if I had known.'

That, of course, was the answer to the other matter that had been puzzling for some time. She knew when *UB-44* was due back from patrol because Gorst tipped her off from his own sources of information. He had not warned her this time because he had thought the trap was secure and that Bergman would be under arrest within hours of returning.

'I've been doing some reading of French naval history,' Bergman told her casually.

Michelle frowned and then laughed. 'Did you learn anything, cheri?'

'I learned that there was no submarine called *Le Plongeur*. And, more importantly, there was no such person as Jules Lamartine.'

Michelle's face suddenly paled. Her hand went to her throat. But her mind was a complete blank. Why the hell had Gorst given her a cover story that could be blown by merely looking up a few records. Obviously he, and everyone else, had underestimated *UB-44*'s skipper. And why was the *Kapitanleutnant* free to walk the streets of Lorient? Gorst had phoned to warn her that his immediate scheme had failed but he had given her no indication how or why - just that, next time she slept with Bergman, she was to pump him about his life in Kiel. And his old girlfriends.

Konrad stared at her with cold, determined eyes. He noted her immaculate beauty, the flawless skin, the carefully brushed blonde hair. And he remembered how Rahel had looked after Gorst had finished with her. He felt suddenly calm and confident as he did in the control room of *UB-44* before going into action. Bergman had never struck a woman before. But there was always a first time for everything.

NINE

'Will you give me your word that you are fit enough?'

Vice Admiral Doenitz was proud of the fatherly relationship he enjoyed with his U-boat commanders and the sharp edge to the question only served to mask his inner concern. Bergman had always been one of his favourites and the searching grey eyes reflected the worry in his heart. Too many young U-boat captains had driven themselves to exhaustion in what Churchill had aptly described as 'this war of groping and drowning' and a tired commander rarely survived.

'I'm quite fit, sir.'

Doenitz glanced down at the green coloured K/89 report form on his desk.

'*Kapitan* Walther apparently does not agree. He has recommended you for six week's recuperation leave at the Ouiberon rest camp. *Oberleutnant* von Knebel will be taking *UB-44* on its next patrol.'

'But the doctor passed me as fit at the medical, sir,' Bergman protested.

'And how many bottles of champagne did it cost you,

Kapitanleutnant?' Doenitz had also been a U-boat skipper in his time and he knew all the tricks.

Bergman smiled but made no effort to deny the suggestion of bribery. In fact the Flotilla Surgeon had been so shocked by his condition that the price had been placed unexpectedly high.

'With respect, sir, may I ask you to cancel the Flotilla Commander's order. You know as well as I do how many good boats and experienced crews have been lost on their first patrol with a new captain. *UB-44* is my boat, sir. And I have a responsibility to my men.'

The premonition of disaster had haunted Bergman for days and he sensed that *UB-44* would never return from her next mission. The men were as exhausted as he was. And if they were to die he wanted to be with them at the end.

His old fire and enthusiasm had gone and only the flickering flame of duty kept him going. He had been betrayed by those he had trusted and was fighting a war he had come to hate, for a cause he despised. Rahel was under sentence of death and, in all probability, the Gestapo would be waiting for him when he got back. Gorst would certainly demand his revenge for what he had done to Michelle.

There was no clear plan of action in his mind. He was too tired to think. But he was determined that *UB-44*'s next patrol would be a suicide mission destined to bring honour and glory to the tarnished reputation of the *Kriegsmarine.* In death he could perhaps do something to balance the crimes of Germany's leaders. In a way he saw it as an act of atonement for his own sins - a sacrifice to the gods for his murderous attack on the *Koenig* in the days when he still regarded orders as inviolate. But those days had gone. And it was only when he saw Rahel in the hands of the Gestapo that the truth had finally registered in his mind.

Now she was gone too and there was no future to live for. And somewhere on board *UB-44* was a traitor. It was best for everyone that they should all go to the bottom together in glory.

'Very well, Bergman, I will countermand *Kapitan* Walter's orders,' Doenitz told him. 'But von Knebel will sail with you as Executive Officer. I cannot take the risk of your cracking up again.'

'Thank you, sir.'

'And by the way,' the Vice Admiral smiled, 'I hope you are not superstitious. Our combat schedule has you starred to leave Lorient on the 13th.'

Who the hell cares, thought Bergman. They were doomed any way. The despondent expression on his face was misinterpreted by Doenitz.

'Don't look so worried, *Kapitanleutnant*,' he urged as Bergman picked up his cap. 'When I was serving with the Cattaro Flotilla in T 8 we had a foolproof scheme for avoiding the 13th. We used to store ship a day early and leave base on the evening of the 12th. Then we anchored on the far side of the bay overnight and set off the next morning. In that way we obeyed orders but we really left to start our patrol on the 12th. And, believe it or not, we didn't lose a single boat.'

'Thank you, sir. I'll bear your suggestion in mind,' Bergman told him. But he didn't make his assurance sound very convincing. As the *Kapitanleutnant* saluted and went out through the door Doenitz was left with the uneasy feeling that he was watching the departure of a dead man. Then, shaking the mood from his mind,

Germany's U-boat chief busied himself with paperwork again.

Despite his dark forebodings of doom, Bergman chose to follow the Vice Admiral's suggestion and as dusk deepened over the harbour on the evening of the 12th *UB-44* slipped quietly out of the U-boat pens. So far as the men were concerned it was a routine departure. Only the skipper and the new Executive Officer, von Knebel, knew they were leaving twelve hours too early.

The faithful minesweeper mothered them to the mouth of the estuary and Bergman stared up at the bright canopy of stars swinging in the night sky as *UB-44* whispered gently through the smooth water. Suddenly he became aware of a rumbling noise mingling with the steady throb of the engines and, looking aft he saw the searchlights of the port defences stab into the sky. A moment later the crash of the flak barrage hammered in his ears. The *Enemy Aircraft* warning flashing from the bridge of the escort ship was superfluous in the circumstances but he ordered an appropriate acknowledgement.

Ugly flashes of flame illuminated the darkened town as the bombs screamed down on the U-boat pens and the sky was scattered with pin-prick blobs of yellow fire as the flak shells exploded amongst the raiders. A. violent mid-air explosion and a trail of fire spiraling to earth signified the death of one bomber and, as if encouraged by its success, the flak barrage redoubled in venom. Bergman noted without undue surprise that Goering's night-fighters were conspicuous by their absence but, as a naval base, Lorient could scarcely expect the support of the Luftwaffe.

Leaving von Knebel to steer *UB-44* down the swept channel that zig-zagged dangerously through the minefields protecting the inner approaches to the harbour Bergman leaned on the rail at the after end of the bridge lost in his thoughts as he stared astern at the bomb blasted town. This was bad enough but, from rumours that he'd heard, the raids on Germany were a hundred times worse.

He was still a little surprised that Gorst had taken no further action against him after finding Michelle. But, as he was beginning to learn, even the Gestapo needed some evidence to support their charges and the protection of his naval uniform prevented them from arresting him on suspicion and then beating a confession out of him. And it was always possible that Michelle had not dared to tell Gorst the truth. It was not much recommendation when the victim of an *agent provocateur* sees through the disguise and metes out summary justice. And in all probability Michelle was as much in fear of the *Gruppenfuehrer* as everyone else.

'Belle lie a'starboard!'

Wrenching himself away from the rail *UB-44's* skipper joined von Knebel at the forward end of the conning- tower.

'Stop engines. Stand by to dive.'

The lookouts hurried below leaving the two officers alone on the darkened bridge.

'Seems like Doenitz was right when he suggested we sailed tonight,' von Knebel observed. 'I wouldn't like to get caught in that lot.'

Bergman shrugged. 'The pens are quite safe - I doubt if the enemy will ever produce a bomb capable of smashing through all that concrete. Not unless he can find some way of cracking the atom or something.'

'I know the boats are safe enough,' von Knebel agreed. 'I was thinking of the crews who might be out in the town on leave. The way things are going we need trained men more than new submarines.'

Well here are another forty they'll have to replace soon, Bergman thought to himself. But he merely nodded his agreement to von Knebel's sentiments. Why tell the poor bastard he was going to die soon. Standing by the hatch he waited as the Executive Officer slid down the ladder.

'I intend to rest on the bottom overnight,' he explained as he clipped the lower hatch. 'So just flood up and let her sink.'

The main vents opened to admit the sea into the empty ballast tanks and, with her buoyancy destroyed by the growing weight of water, UB-44 sank slowly and silently beneath the water with dead engines. There was a gentle bump at eighty feet and the U-boat settled into her bed of mud with an imperceptible lurch.

'Stop flooding.'

Herzog reached up and twisted the valve wheels shut while Riedel walked slowly round the control room checking the instruments.

'All secured, sir,' he reported and Bergman nodded.

'Very good, Riedel. Tell all hands to stand down and get a good night's sleep.' He paused for a moment. 'And tell them that this time it's going to be something big.'

Bergman took it easy on the outward leg of the patrol, letting von Knebel run the boat while he gathered his strength for the coming battle. What lay ahead of them he did not know. But he was determined that UB-44 would sell her life dearly. Most of his crew were young men without families. And of the handful of veterans who sailed with him on every patrol the majority, so far as he knew, were unmarried. The others had lived good full lives. And no U-boat man could expect to live forever. Better to die now while Germany was still victorious than later when the seeds of defeat had blossomed into the misery of despair, revolution, and occupation.

Sitting alone in the wardroom he wondered whether his father had experienced the same premonition of impending doom when *UC-115* had crept out of Zeebrugge on its last patrol in January 1918. It was strange how, at moments like this, his thoughts always turned to his father. It was almost as if his spirit sailed in *UB-44* to guide and protect him.

But Bergman was forced to admit that, even if he did, his ghostly presence had brought the U-boat little success so far on this patrol. The hoodoo of doom hung heavy over the worn-out submarine as her plates groaned and strained with every roll. She was six months overdue for a refit and now, each time she dug her nose into the mid-Atlantic swell, she complained bitterly in a language that only the seamen could understand. Each day brought its regular quota of fresh leaks as the Krupp steel plates, weakened by the stress of ten combat patrols, yielded wearily to the relentless battering of the sea. And short circuits, often spectacular displays of green and blue sparks, occurred almost hourly and brought the electrical artificers cursing from their bunks to carry our makeshift repairs.

But, most disquieting of all, leaking fuel from a fractured oil pipe had contaminated *UB-44's* fresh water tanks forcing Bergman to introduce an immediate rationing system. And washing, a luxury even at the best of times, was strictly forbidden. Soon the sickly sweet smell of human sweat dominated the cramped interior of the U-boat with a stomach-churning pungency that even overwhelmed the usual reek of diesel oil and stale cabbage water.

War Diary: 24 May 1941 Patrol Day 12. Still no sightings. Weather dull. 8/10ths cloud, wind force 6 from NE. Heavy surface swell. Starboard diesel out of service for three hours but now repaired. Last known position (04-00 hrs) 36°21'W; 48°14'N. Course 240 at 7 knots. Bergman K/L

Von Knebel handed over the watch to Riedel and slid down thankfully into the warmth of the control room. The stench made his stomach heave after the fresh salt air on the bridge but it was preferable to the biting cold of the exposed conning-tower. Throwing off his wet oilskins he ducked through the bulkhead hatch and pushed aside the curtains into the wardroom. Bergman, still immersed in his morbid thoughts, did not look up but continued staring blankly at the book open on the table in front of him.

'Riedel has taken over, sir,' von Knebel reported as he went across to the eternal coffee pot bubbling on the electric ring in the comer. 'You're down to relieve him at the end of the forenoon watch but I'll stand in for you if you wish.'

Bergman stirred himself reluctantly. He shook his head. 'Thank you, von Knebel, but I'll take my turn. Some fresh air will probably do me good.'

The Executive Officer detected a flatness in the skipper's voice that heralded a return of the depression that had held him in its inexorable grip for most of the patrol. It was like a dead man speaking. No spark of life. No hope. Von Knebel shot a quick glance across the wardroom to confirm his suspicions. Bergman was sitting hunched in his chair, his eyes dull, staring at the claustrophobic steel walls of their submerged vault.

'Should be setting course for home soon, sir,' he reminded the skipper quietly. 'Korman reported our fuel stocks down to twenty-three tons. I make us about nine hundred miles from Lorient so we'll have to head back within the next forty-eight hours at the latest - and even that's cutting it a bit fine.'

Bergman looked up sharply. 'We stay on patrol, *Oberleutnant*,' he said coldly. 'I will decide when we return to base.'

'But, sir, we need at least fifteen tons plus a twenty-five per cent reserve ...'

'Silence!' Bergman's eyes blazed fiercely. His threshold of irritability was dangerously low and even a rational proposition could trigger off a towering rage if it did not accord exactly with his personal views. Rising to his feet he began pacing the caged confines of the wardroom. '*UB-44.* will gain a glorious victory on this patrol, von Knebel. Mark my words. And we stay in the patrol area until we find a target - even if we run clean out of fuel in the process.'

Who the devil does he think he is, von Knebel wondered, the skipper of the Flying Dutchman? Walther had been right - Bergman was teetering on the edge of a complete breakdown. And although he had received no specific instructions von Knebel knew that, at some point in time, he would have to take over command of *UB-44* and usurp the captain's authority. The question was -

when? Perhaps right now, while Bergman was at his most irrational, would be best. At least the crew would understand the reason for his action. And that was another aspect of the problem. From what he had seen so far, several senior members of the crew were damn nearly as mad as their commander. But it had to be done or *UB-44* would join the growing list of submarines written off as *'missing presumed lost'*. Taking a deep breath the Executive Officer put down his coffee cup and rose to his feet.

'Urgent radio message, sir!'

Both officers turned as Drache thrust his head through the curtains clutching the signal slip. Bergman held out his hand and the wireless operator handed it to him obediently. Von Knebel allowed his taught nerves to unwind. He wondered how long it would be before he found enough courage to challenge the captain again. Certainly, for the moment, the opportunity had passed.

'It's in English, sir,' Drache pointed out. 'I picked up an enemy transmitter a few minutes ago. I can't read it properly but, if I've got it right, it's hot!'

Bergman glanced down at the paper. His command of English was good and the gloom lifted from his face as he translated the signal. His eyes suddenly became alive and his mouth was smiling as he looked up at von Knebel.

'*Bismark* and *Prinz Eugen* have broken out into the North Atlantic through the Denmark Strait. A British Admiralty communique has reported the *Hood* sunk by gunfire and *Prince of Wales* seriously damaged.' His face glowed with excitement and the lassitude and despair of the previous week fell away like snow melting in the summer sun. 'This is what I've been waiting for von Knebel. I knew our luck would change. The Royal Navy will pour every available ship into the Atlantic to hunt down the *Bismarck* - and we'll be smack bang in the middle waiting for them!'

Bergman hurried out of the wardroom into the control room to announce the news of *Bismarck's* success to the men over *UB-44's* loudspeaker system. Its effect was immediate and electrifying. Drooping shoulders lifted and dull eyes found a new sparkle. What a colossal victory! Who could claim that Britannia ruled the waves now.

'*Steuermann* — course 0-4-0! Engine room - full ahead both!'

UB-44 swung on to her new course and a plume of spray stung back from the bows as the diesels drove her northwards at flank speed.

'Still worried about the fuel shortage, *Oberleutnant*?' Bergman taunted his Executive Officer with a laugh.

'No, sir. If we run out of oil we'll just have to get back on the batteries. In fact I'd bloody well paddle her home if necessary.'

The atmosphere of despondent gloom had vanished at the thought of action. Every man on the U-boat was anxious to do his utmost. And even *UB-44* seemed on her best behaviour as she sped north. Sprung plates that had previously leaked continuously suddenly sealed off and became watertight of their own accord and even the electrical artificers no longer cursed when circuits shorted under the heavy loads which the skipper was subjecting them to.

Daylight whispered into dusk and the dark of night descended swiftly, but *UB-44* continued hammering northwards at undiminished speed, while a stream of signals from *BdU* crackled into the radio room. *Ark Royal* was known to be coming up from Gibraltar with Force H and, just before midnight, the carrier *Victorious* was reported approaching *Bismarck* in heavy mist. Bergman marked each sighting report on his chart as he weighed up his best line of attack. The German heavy units were too far north to consider close co-operation but it was becoming increasingly obvious that an important British force must pass in the vicinity of *UB-* *44's* probable track during the next twelve hours.

And, at 07-00 the next morning, Drache handed him the signal he had been waiting for.

MOST IMMEDIATE

06-31. 23-3-41. *BdU* *to* *all* *U-boat* *commanders in Squares MX-14 & MX-13. U-302 reports carrier of Illustrious class with four destroyers on NE by E course. Speed 28 knots. All units attack. Repeat attack.*

Doenitz BdU

Bergman studied the chart carefully. *UB-44* was in the northern* sector of Square MX-14. Checking his other data he marked a faint penciled cross on the point where he thought the carrier had been sighted. Then he ruled off a NE by E course. It passed within five miles of their present DR position!

Grabbing a piece of paper he quickly calculated speeds and distances, opened up the dividers, and marked off his estimate of the carrier group's present location. It was all guesswork, but it was a chance worth taking. With a final glance at the chart Bergman took his vital decision.

'Steer three points to port! Stand by for action stations

in one hour.' He lifted the bridge telephone. 'Clear the conning-tower, Number Two, and prepare to dive!'

UB-44, rust-streaked and battle-weary, was just eight hours into the 13th day of her patrol.

High up on the flying-control bridge of HMS *Arrogant* the Commander (Flying) watched anxiously as the first subflight of Swordfish torpedo bombers was trundled off the lifts by the deck handling party and wheeled towards the stem. Visibility at sea level was still little more than a mile and although the wind was barely more than a light breeze, the sea was steep. And, as if to underline his fears, the carrier dipped her blunt nose into a trough and then reared upwards like an unbroken horse trying to unseat its rider. How any pilot could take off in such adverse conditions was a complete mystery and yet *Ark Royal,* only two hundred miles to the north in similar weather, had already reported the successful launch of her first strike. So it had to be possible.

Pacing the navigating bridge one level higher than flying control, *Arrogant's* skipper, Captain Roebuck, DSO, had other worries. Sherwood, commanding officer of the starboard escort destroyer had picked up an asdic contact five minutes earlier, and was already circling away from the carrier in search of the U-boat. Like most aircraft carriers *Arrogant* was especially vulnerable to torpedo attack and Roebuck knew that their chances of survival in this sea were minimal if they were hit. And if *Arrogant* were in danger of being torpedoed he had to decide whether the Swordfish Squadron should be launched before it was too late. *Bismarck* must be attacked with everything the Royal Navy could throw at her and there seemed no point in losing nine valuable torpedo bombers as well as their mother ship.

He picked up the red telephone that connected the bridge to Flying Control.

'*Pelican* has reported a U-boat contact. What is our latest target distance?'

'Five hundred miles, sir.'

'Could Three Squadron get back if they were launched now?'

'Not a chance, sir. Maximum endurance is seven hundred and fifty miles.'

Roebuck paused and looked down at the six biplanes arrowed in position on the broad flight deck below. His instincts warned him to wait, but tradition demanded its sacrifice. Better to lose six bombers after the attack than before.

'But you can reach *Bismarck*?'

'Yes, sir. But they'll be down to their reserve tanks if this head wind persists. We'll have no chance of recovering them.'

To hell with recovery. The important thing was their ability to reach and hit the target. Much as he hated to face the unpalatable fact - the Swordfish were expendable. Roebuck made his decision.

'Direct them to locate *Ark Royal* or *Victorious* for recovery. Get them launched as quickly as you can.'

Arrogant flashed a warning signal to the destroyer screen as she turned into the wind ready for launching. The bows smashed down into the head sea and a wall of water, rising to the height of the flight deck, broke in a fury of white spray as it struck the curving underside of the deck. The Swordfish were spotted too far aft to be affected but nevertheless the sight of the sea bursting up over the bows was sufficient to daunt even the most determined pilot.

'She's lifting at least thirty feet on each crest, sir,' Armstrong reported back to the Flight Leader in the rear cockpit. 'When we get the "wave off" I'm going to start my take-off run as the bows go down — I think I've got the timing right. She'll be rising again by the time we're halfway down the flight deck and we should get maximum elevation at lift-off point.'

'Okay, Jimmy. I leave the flying to you. My job doesn't start until we're up. So you'd better make it or I'll be joining the ranks of the unemployed.'

Huddled miserably at his exposed station midway down the starboard side, Lieutenant Chard, *Arrogant*'s 'batsman' received Davidson's 'okay for take-off' and clambered up on to the slippery flight deck. His arms wagged up and down and the propeller of *Blue Titty Rita* dissolved to a silver blur as Armstrong gunned the Bristol Pegasus engine to life. Streaks of yellow flame flashed from the exhaust and he raised his arm as a stand-by signal to the men holding the chocks. *Arrogant* crested another wave, hung precariously in the air for a moment, and then plunged her bows into the trough that followed with a plate-shuddering thud. Armstrong's arm snapped down and *Blue Titty Rita* catapulted down the narrow flight deck as the chocks were jerked away from the wheels.

It was like a nightmare ride down the Cresta Run on a runaway bobsleigh. Water sprayed from the wheels and the Swordfish hurtled downhill gathering speed with every passing yard. Peering out through the half circle of his windscreen Phillips could see the end of the deck looming ahead and the wild black sea beyond. He wanted to close his eyes but forced himself to watch. Thank God

Jimmy Armstrong was in the pilot's seat. He wouldn't have trusted anyone else.

Arrogant hit the bottom of the trough as the Swordfish flashed level with the island superstructure to starboard. Then, groaning with effort, her bows began to rise. *Blue Titty Rita's* engine screamed at full stretch and the airspeed indicator trembled at sixty-five knots. The tail wheel lifted and they seemed to be racing up a vast steel hill. Then the landing-wheels left the deck, the Swordfish's wings wobbled slightly as Armstrong corrected the angle of take-off - and they were away and climbing hard into the dark clouds that grumbled ominously above the ship.

Two more aircraft followed, staggering precariously into the sky as they clawed wildly for air-speed at the end of the run. But the pilot of the fourth Swordfish, *M-for-Mike,* misjudged the heaving pitch of the flight deck and vanished over the bows into the foaming sea below with a screech of brakes. Number Five, too, came to grief as an unexpected gust of wind veered her to starboard and sent her crashing into the barrier.

Roebuck's expression did not alter as he witnessed the two accidents. Lifting the telephone he ordered Davidson to suspend further operations before the last of the torpedo bombers started down the flight deck. Tradition may have demanded sacrifices. But not suicide.

'Torpedoes! Red - 9 — zero!'

Arrogant's captain swung to the starboard windows of the navigating bridge. Two bubbling white wakes were arrowing towards the carrier's bows at an acute angle.

'Hard a'port!'-

The torpedoes, moving at forty-five knots, were barely four hundred yards away and there was a nail-biting pause as the carrier hesitated before answering the helm. Three hundred yards.

Roebuck sensed the bows beginning to turn - slowly at first and then more sharply. He looked down at the torpedo tracks and saw the angle opening as the carrier swung out of danger. Then, suddenly, they had passed clear of the bows and were disappearing out of view on the far side. Thank God the enemy were using the old-type 'heater' torpedoes that left a visible wake. They'd have stood no chance against the new electric models that left virtually no telltale track on the surface.

Peering out to starboard through the bridge windows he wondered whether Sherwood had obtained a positive contact with the U-boat.

Ping-ping... ping-ping... ping-ping. .,

'Asdic range two miles, sir. Contact positive.'

Lieutenant-Commander Sherwood nodded as he stared into the mist ahead. Visibility was about two miles - not much for a U-boat search. But if Jerry stayed below the surface they had him cold. And if the bastard tried to come up and run for it, *Pelican's* D/R radar would locate him immediately.

The torpedo tracks had been an unexpected gift from, the gods. The Germans must be having supply problems if they were still kitting their U-boats out with the old-type 'hot: air' fish. Or maybe this particular commander was just unlucky. It had been a bad shot in any event - fired too soon and from the wrong angle. Herr U-boat Kapitan must be getting jumpy or he was a new boy learning the trade. Still it had been a close-run thing and Roebuck had demonstrated his superb seamanship swinging *Arrogant* clear as quickly as he did.

Ping-ping ... ping-ping . .. ping-ping ... The double

pulse, indicating a positive contact with an underwater object, echoed monotonously in his right ear as the sound was relayed to the repeater loudspeaker on the bridge Sherwood leaned forward over the rail frowning. It seemed odd that the U-boat was taking no evasive action. The double pulse had held steady for more than a minute and the bubbling white wake from *Pelican's* stem was irrefutable evidence that the destroyer was maintaining a dead straight course.

'Yeoman! Take a signal for *Perciv al* ... signal reads: Reduce to half speed and hold course. I will over-run target and attack from reciprocal bearing.'

Leading Signaller Collins sighted the Aldis lamp astern, called up their Division mate, and began clicking the shutters in a series of 'long-and-shorts'. A shaded blue light replied from the bridge of *Percival* and her bow wave fell away as she lost speed.

'Signal acknowledged and understood, sir.'

Sherwood nodded. 'Coxswain, I want you to circle out to starboard and come back on a reverse course. Understood?'

Understood, sir.'

'Turning in two minutes — stand-by.'

Thrusting through the water at thirty-five knots, *Pelican* was rapidly opening the distance from the destroyer astern and Sherwood looked sharply up to port to see if *Arrogant* was still in sight. The ungainly bulk of the carrier loomed indistinctly through the mist, but she was moving safely away from danger. That was one less headache to worry about. But the persistent and unvarying course of the enemy submarine puzzled *Pelican's*,skipper.

There seemed to be only one explanation of the U-boat's odd behaviour — and that didn't bear thinking about. Was the submarine acting as a decoy to lure him away from the carrier so that a second U-boat, whose presence was so far undetected, could get an easy shot at *Arrogant*. Perhaps that was why they had deliberately fired the old pattern torpedoes — scenting a false trail away from their prime target by means of the bubbling torpedo tracks on the surface. Certainly no U-boat skipper in his right mind would maintain speed and course so blatantly when he knew his boat was being hunted by destroyers. It was asking for trouble.

'Ten seconds, cox'n ... stand by. Hard a'starboard!' Chief Petty Officer Larwood swung the wheel and *Pelican* heeled sharply in response to the rudder. Lying over with her starboard rails kissing the sea, the destroyer circled in a sharp turn. And crouching aft at their stations on the quarter deck, the depth-charge crews clung desperately to lifelines as their feet slipped on the wet steel plating while, deep below, there was a clatter of saucepans in the galley and an angry roar from the chief cook.

Pelican was now running bows-on into the swell and she took the sea green over the foc'sl'e as the stem sliced into a wall of black water. But Sherwood held the destroyer into her tight turn and, as the sea came on to the beam, she seemed to lean even more precariously. Heavy steel staunchions bent like soft metal rods and with a sharp crack, the starboard whaler ripped from its davits, shattered itself into splinters against the superstructure, and swirled astern in a raging flood of water.

Suddenly the destroyer straightened up and the worst was over. Sherwood stared down at the standard compass, watched the needle line up, and turned to the cox'n.

'Midships helm, Chief. Steady as she goes.'

'Midships, sir.'

'Half ahead both.' *Pelican* slowed in response to the order and the men on the bridge sensed that the skipper was closing in for the kill. Yet, aside from the monotonous doubleecho from the asdic, it could have been no more than a tense moment in a peace-time training exercise. And there was certainly no visible evidence of the U-boat lurking beneath the surface somewhere between the two converging destroyers.

'For'ard gun crews close up! Set depth-charges for one hundred feet and remove safety pins.'

Pelican was ready for action. Stripped and prepared for battle like a fighting cock waiting to be thrown into the ring. Sherwood stared ahead watching his division mate. Suddenly two black objects catapulted from the stem of *Percival* raced gracefully through the air, and dropped back into the water with a plunging splash. A fraction of a second later the men on *Pelican's* bridge heard the dull thud of the depth- charge mortar's detonating charge. Less than half a mile separated the two destroyers and both held their head-on courses at a steady fifteen knots.

CRUM-M-P! CRUM-M-P! The sea astern of *Percival* heaved as if torn by an underwater volcanic eruption. Two white circles of foam rose to the surface and, seconds later, a pair of enormous geysers of dirty-grey water spewed high into the air as the depth-charges exploded. Almost before the sea had subsided two more canisters hurtled into the air, described a sharp parabola, and slipped quietly back into the depths. Sherwood leaned forward intently as he waited for the explosions. This was the kill. He was sure of it.

CRUM-M-P! CRUM-M-P!

'Full ahead both!'

It was jumping the gun but *Pelican's* skipper knew it was going to happen.

And it did. As the sea erupted again with the blasting detonation of the second pair of depth-charges, there was a sudden froth of air bubbles on the surface midway between the two widening circles of tormented water and the grey, rust-streaked bows of a U-boat emerged at a steep angle.

Pelican was barely two hundred yards away and her razor- sharp bows were cleaving the water at thirty-five knots in response to Sherwood's demand for maximum power.

'Starboard the helm, cox'n. Aim for the conning-tower!'

Everything now depended on Larwood's experienced hands. There was nothing more Sherwood could do. He had wound *Pelican* up to full speed at exactly the right moment and, basing his decision on an intuition firmly grounded on centuries of tradition, he had judged the U-boat's probable position to within fifty yards. Now he could only pray that the enemy would not slip from the trap at the last minute.

'Hang on, chaps!' he warned the other men on the bridge. 'There's going to be a bloody great crunch at any moment.'

Pelican's bows cut into the thin plating of the U-boat's hull just forward of the conning-tower with a crash of metal and a shriek of torn steel. *UB-44* rolled violently to starboard under the impact as the destroyer rode up on top of its victim forcing it down into the sea. The dull red anti-rust paint covering the submarine's exposed ballast tanks resembled a stain of blood along its side and, like a celluloid duck striving to return to the surface of a child's bath, *UB-44* twisted violently under the destroyer's keel and bobbed up again on *Pelican's* port beam.

The great gash in the plating was clear for all to see. The periscopes and other equipment of the conning-tower were crushed and bent where the destroyer's keel had dragged across it. Thick black oil gushed from a ruptured fuel pipe and a stream of air bubbles from the bows pinpointed a fracture in the pressure hull.

UB-44 pitched and rolled forlornly. Then her bows suddenly dipped beneath the surface, her stem rose high out of the water to expose her propellers, and she dived towards the bottom.

'Poor bastards,' Sherwood said quietly. 'What a way to die.'

'Shall we send them on their way with a couple of ash-cans, sir?'

Pelican's skipper hesitated. The U-boat was finished. Of that he was quite certain. But there was no harm in making sure. Germany's sea wolves rarely showed mercy to their victims - they could hardly expect any now in the moment of defeat. He nodded.

'Go ahead, Gunner. Fire one pattern of four. He's done for anyway.'

Exactly thirty seconds later four towering fountains of water erupted from astern of *Pelican* as the depth-charges detonated a hundred feet below the grey surface of the heaving ocean. To the men on the destroyer's bridge they looked for all the world like four ghostly white tombstones marking the grave of the unfortunate *UB-44*.

TEN

The scene inside *UB-44*. as she sank beneath the surface was one of complete chaos. The violence of the impact had shattered the lights and the claustrophobic darkness added a new dimension of horror to the fears of the trapped men. Their ears were deafened by the shrill scream of compressed air escaping from the fractured pressure lines, the acrid stink of smouldering rubber choked in their throats, and the sound of water flooding into the crippled U-boat only served to compound their initial panic.

'Emergency stations! Blow all tanks - hydroplanes hard a'rise!'

Bergman's voice brought the men to their senses and gave them a focal point of hope in the frightening darkness. Above all, the sharp edge to the command steadied their nerves. Groping forward blindly, and stumbling over the debris that littered the deck, they moved to their emergency stations. Further aft in the black vault of the motor room someone reached into the smouldering mess of bumt-out fuses, isolated the switch, and turned on the reserve power supply. The glow from the lamps was disappointingly feeble but it was sufficient to see by, and the sight of the skipper calmly checking off the damage helped to restore the men's confidence.

Blood was dripping from Bergman's cheek where he had been thrown against the sharp metal edge of a fuse box but he seemed oblivious of his injury and he gave the impression — quite deliberately — of being in complete control of the situation. Whatever the state of his mind during that final nerve-shattering hunt by the enemy destroyers, or the bitter disappointment he had suffered when *UB-44*'s torpedoes had missed the carrier, the terrifying crash of *Pelican's* bows biting deep into the U-boat's fragile hull had reawakened his old instinct for survival. And the fatalistic acceptance of death that had bemused his brain since the day he had seen Rahel in the hands of the Gestapo was swept clear by the nightmare danger that now faced him and his crew. Everything now depended on himself. And he did not intend to fail in his trust.

Compressed air hissed through the blowing lines as the U- boat struggled to regain positive buoyancy but, despite the frantic efforts of her crew, *UB-44* showed a stubborn reluctance to rise.

'Fifty feet and sinking, sir!'

Bergman glanced at the shattered glass of the depth gauge. The Second Coxswain was right. They were sinking. Something was making the U-boat bow-heavy. That could mean only one thing - *Pelican's* attack had inflicted mortal damage and they were slowly flooding. As if to confirm his fears *Torpedomechaniker* Schoemann staggered through the forward bulkhead door and collapsed face down on the deck of the control room. Herzog rolled him over on to his back. His overalls were soaking wet and his eyes stared wide with horror as he struggled to speak.

'The bow torpedo compartment is flooding, sir...'

Bergman bent over him. 'Pedersen and Schomberg? Where are they?'

'They stayed behind to secure the watertight door, sir. It's jammed.'

Bergman passed the exhausted man over to *Sanitasobermaat* Steiner while he considered the significance of the Schoemann's report. The situation was apparently worse than he had originally feared. If the sea were entering the forward compartment it meant that the pressure hull was fractured - no wonder the bows were heavy.

'Close all watertight doors!'

That was the obvious thing to do. Escape was impossible for the present and the doors would at least stop the sea from roaring relentlessly through the length of the boat. And keep those tanks blowing - that was the other main task. But after that? Bergman knew that before he could take any further decisions he needed an expert assessment of the damage. He nodded to von Knebel.

'Take two men to check the situation for'ard *Oberleutnant*. And take a runner with you to bring me a preliminary report. Let me know if we can plug the leaks.'

Von Knebel selected three seamen; the party climbed through the forward watertight door and started towards the bows. Herzog swung the heavy counter-weighted hatch shut and secured it firmly with the locking bar. If the Executive Officer and his party were trapped by the rising water that was one of the accepted risks of the job.

'Seventy feet, sir.'

CRUM-M-P! CRUM-M-P! The first depth charges threw *UB-44,* violently to starboard with a spine-snapping kick that hurled every man inside the submarine against the unyielding steel plates with bruising force.

'Bastards!' someone spat out.

'They're just making sure of a kill,' another voice explained objectively as if he were watching the scene in a cinema.

Bergman braced himself as he detected the ominous double click of hydrostatic valves opening. The next pair of depth-charges must be bloody close to hear that, he thought to himself. It was like seeing a flash of lightning and waiting for the thunderclap when one was a child.

CRUM-M-P! CRUM-M-P! A giant's hammer struck the outer hull twice in quick succession and the angry reverberations echoed through the U-boat like a death knell. *UB- 44* tilted sharply to port and the emergency lights flickered and died. Men cursed and swore anonymously in the sudden darkness as the concussion of the double explosion threw them across the narrow width of the submarine for the second time. Shattered glass tinkled to the floor and loose equipment bounced and rattled on the steel deck like tin cans being kicked down an empty alley.

Bergman felt the U-boat heel over, hesitate, and then straighten up again. The stench of burning rubber had worsened as another series of electrical circuits had shortened and more frighteningly, he sensed that the inrush of water at the bow end of the boat was increasing. The emergency lighting came on again as *Mechanikergefreiter* Petz replaced the fuses and Bergman stared round to assess the extent of the further damage they had suffered. The interior of the submarine was now a complete shambles and cork packing from the overhead seams floated gently down like a brown snowstorm, covering every surface with a fine crumbly dust that irritated the eyes and blocked the nose.

'Eighty feet and sinking, sir,' Giesse reported gloomily. 'Keep blowing. Damage control parties report please.'

A loud hammering distracted Bergman's attention and he turned anxiously.

'Permission to open the hatch, sir?' Herzog called. 'It's the Executive Officer and his party.'

'Check for flooding first, Cox'n.'

Herzog peered through the armoured glass grill in the circular door and shone his torch inside.

'No sign of water, sir.'

'Right! Open up and let them in.'

The Coxswain dragged the locking bar clear and pulled the handle down. The heavy door swung open and the exhausted men tumbled through one by one. Thrusting the hatch shut as the last man clambered through the circular opening, Herzog quickly secured it and slid the locking bar home. The *Oberleutnant*'s party looked all in; von Knebel was clutching his right arm tight against his body and biting his lip to counteract the pain.

'All secure for'ard, sir,' he reported. 'The torpedo compartment is flooded but Number One bulkhead door is shut and latched. There are numerous water leaks in the second compartment and one section of plating looks likely to collapse at any moment - that's why we got out in a hurry.' 'What about Pedersen and Schomberg?'

'Trapped in the torpedo flat, sir. They volunteered to go into the bow compartment and close the door from the inside.' The Executive Officer paused for a moment. 'They knew we would have to abandon them there - there was no chance of getting them out.'

Bergman nodded. It was the sort of selfless sacrifice that had to be made when a submarine was facing disaster. If they hadn't sealed off the bulkhead *UB-44.* would have been flooded from end to end by now. He suddenly remembered Otto Kretschmer explaining an identical situation to him when he was a cadet on board *U-23.* In fact he could still recall every word as vividly as the day Kretschmer had spoken them:

'A U-boat is divided into a series of watertight compartments and these doors form the seal that cuts each off from the other. In an emergency, if the boat is holed and water is coming in, it is the duty of every man to close the door nearest to him even if, by doing so, he traps himself on the wrong side of the hatch inside the flooding compartment.'

Well Pedersen and Schomberg had done their duty. And now it was up to him to see that their sacrifice was not in vain.

'*Oberleutnant* von Knebel's arm is broken, sir.'

Steiner was bending over the Executive Officer and the urgency of his voice broke into Bergman's thoughts.

'Can you fix it, *Sanitasobermaat?*'

'It's a bad break,' Steiner said doubtfully. 'I'd have to put him out while I reset the bones.'

Von Knebel was the one man above all others that Bergman needed in the present dire emergency. With the Executive Officer gone he was left only with young Riedel. And that meant relying on the unpredictable Herzog.

'How long will it take?'

'Twenty to thirty minutes — but he'll be too groggy for duty for several hours afterwards.'

Bergman looked at von Knebel's drawn grey face and

pain-twisted lips. Despite his golden rule that the boat must come first he could not bring himself to leave the *Oberleutnant* in this state. Taking a deep breath he nodded his approval.

'Open the after watertight door and take him into the wardroom,' he told Steiner. 'And report back to me as soon as you have finished.'

Von Knebel grimaced with agony as two of the seamen helped him up off the floor.

'I'm okay, sir,' he protested weakly. 'Steiner can set my arm without doping me to the eye-balls. Give me a bottle of brandy - that's all I need. Then as soon as he's fixed my arm I can come on duty.'

Bergman shook his head. 'We'll have the job done properly, Number One. And that's an order. I can cope on my own — it could be a lot worse.'

'Ninety feet, sir.'

So they were still sinking despite the blowing.

'Motor room!' Bergman waiting at the telephone for the acknowledgement and breathed a silent sigh of relief to find the communications to the stern section still working. 'Korman here, sir.'

'Run the motors full astern. I want to see if we can pull ourselves up by our own power.'

The high-pitched hum of the motors increased as Korman obeyed the order and, still holding the telephone in his hand, Bergman watched the needle of the depth-gauge with the intensity of a gambler watching the roll of the dice during a losing run. It was no use.

'Stop motors - they're having no effect and we'll have to conserve our battery power. What's the situation aft?'

'All secure, sir. No leaks and everything seems as

sound as a bell. We've lost most of our fuel though - the pipes to the bunkers must have fractured.'

Korman sounded cheerful enough; Bergman left him in blissful ignorance of the fatal damage in the fore compartments. The fewer who knew of their dangerous predicament the better. Putting the phone back on its hook he turned to Riedel. The boy's face mirrored the terror in his heart but, forcing his personal fears into the background, he continued steadfastly at his station like the veteran he had become in a few short months of combat operations.

'Take over while I work out our next move,' Bergman told him quietly. 'Keep a special eye on the ballast tanks and if they show any signs of flooding, start blowing them again. Not too much - I've got to conserve our compressed air as long as possible.'

'One hundred feet,' Giesse reported. 'Bow-down angle increased to 30° and we're diving faster.'

I'm glad he had the sense to say 'diving' and not 'sinking' Bergman thought to himself. It didn't sound so bad that way. He nodded but made no comment.

'Cox'n - I want you in the wardroom for a conference.' Herzog acknowledged the unexpected order and Bergman turned back to Riedel. 'Carry on, Number Two. And don't be afraid to give me a shout if conditions alter suddenly.' Steiner was still in the wardroom as the skipper entered and he came to attention dutifully. Von Knebel was lying unconscious on the lower bunk with his right arm carefully splinted. He seemed comfortable enough.

'He should regain consciousness in fifteen minutes or so, sir,' Steiner reported. 'But try to make him stay in his bunk for a while if you can - he'll be feeling fairly groggy.'

'Thank you, Steiner. I'll let you know if we need you. Dismiss.'

Bergman sat down at the wardroom table and motioned Herzog to join him. The time for doubts and suspicions had gone. Whether the Coxswain was a traitor or not was of little consequence when every man on board was facing death. And, as a realist, the *Kapitanleutnant* knew that while von Knebel was out of action Herzog was the only man he could turn to.

'I don't give much for our chances, sir,' the Coxswain observed objectively as soon as Steiner had passed beyond earshot. 'Number Two compartment will be completely flooded inside five minutes.'

'That's what I'm worried about,' Bergman admitted frankly. It was a relief to confide his worries to someone — even an erstwhile murderer. '*UB-44* has a design capability of surfacing with one compartment flooded but, with two gone, there's not enough air in the tanks to restore positive buoyancy. In other words even if we blow all tanks we can't get back to the surface.'

'And so we go on sinking?'

'As things stand at the moment - yes.'

'What's the diving depth of these *Type VIIB* boats, sir?'

'Three hundred feet tested. But she'd probably make four hundred in one piece. After that the hull would be crushed by the pressure of the sea.'

Herzog considered the matter dispassionately for a few moments as he analysed the possibilities. 'What depth of water are we in at present?' he asked finally.

Bergman shrugged.

'We're more or less in mid-Atlantic. I'd say not less than one thousand feet. And probably a good deal more.'

'We were sinking at the rate of ten feet every five minutes when I timed Giesse's reports,' Herzog said, thinking aloud. It's probably double that rate since the hull plates gave way in Number Two. That means we've got...'

'Twenty minutes, Chief. At most, thirty,' Bergman said quietly as he looked up from the calculations he had scribbled on his notepad. 'Our rate of descent has risen to ten feet a minute since Number Two flooded.'

Herzog digested the startling new facts in silence. Just thirty minutes. And then *UB-44.* would be crushed like a fragile egg-shell squeezed in a giant's hand. Those last few minutes would be the worst. Waiting and listening for the hull to crack. Hearing the first groaning creaks of strain as the stressed steel was bent slowly inwards by the inexorable power of the sea - the first faint trickle of water, the scream of tortured plates, the sea pouring in through gaping splits in the hull, and then ...

'We might get gassed first,' he said slowly as if searching for an alternative way to die.

Bergman shrugged. 'If the sea water gets into the battery compartments there's no doubt about it. But I think the hull will break up before the chlorine has a chance to work its way through the boat. At least I hope so. I don't fancy your cheerful alternative.'

The vagaries of the human character were strange, Bergman thought to himself. Yesterday he would have welcomed death. In fact he would have encouraged it. And yet now, faced by its inevitability, he could think only of life and what it held. Not even the knowledge that Rahel was equally close to dying persuaded him to relinquish his tenuous grip on life. If he survived he would avenge her murder a thousand times over. But, if he died, her death like his own would have been in vain.

'I suppose there's nothing we can do, sir,' Herzog asked, even though he knew the inevitable answer before putting the question. 'Should we tell the men.'

Bergman rubbed his hands across his face, massaging his closed eyes with the tips of his fingers, as he tried to think.

A soft thud tremored through the U-boat and he looked up alertly. Something slid and slithered beneath the keel and the awkward bow-down angle eased. Getting up quickly he checked the row of repeater instruments fitted into the bulkhead above his bunk. There was a sudden gleam of hope in his eyes as he turned.

'We've stopped sinking, Cox'n! The depth-gauge is steady at one hundred and eighty feet.'

'How the hell...'

Bergman tried to hide his excitement as he rummaged through the charts lying in the drawer of the wardroom bureau. 'The ocean floor is not absolutely smooth, Cox'n. It's rather like a landscape with plains and mountains and valleys — only covered in water.' His searching hands found the chart he wanted at the bottom of the drawer and, lifting it out, he carried it over to the table and smoothed it flat. Bending over it he found their approximate position when they had launched their abortive attack on *Arrogant* and stabbed his finger triumphantly down on a point some twenty miles to the north-west.

'That's it, Herzog! Where my finger is pointing. The Magellan Ridge. It's like an underwater mountain range rising up from the bottom of the ocean. And, by all the gods we've landed smack bang on top of it.'

The Coxswain squinted down at the chart to confirm

the cause of the skipper's excitement. He was not trained to read *Kriegsmarine* charts but, to anyone familiar with a land map, it was easy enough to pick up the straggling line of the ridge as it weaved like an angry snake through the vast deeps of the central Atlantic. And, glancing at the chart's key, he noted that the ridge was shown as lying between one hundred and fifty and two hundred feet below the surface. It was a terrifyingly small area. Yet *UB-44*, as if striving to do her best for the crew even in her final moments, had found it and sunk like a wounded animal to die on top of its highest crest.

'I suppose we can try flooding up the conning-tower compartment and get out that way - you know, using the bubble of air that builds up under pressure.'

Bergman shook his head. 'Not a chance, Cox'n. We're lying too deep. No one could survive an ascent from nearly two hundred feet - they'd be dead from the bends before they even reached the surface. And that's assuming they hadn't ruptured their lungs meanwhile.'

Herzog sighed and sat down again. 'In that case what the hell was the good of landing on the ridge?' he demanded. 'Better we'd gone straight down and got it over with.'

'Time, Cox'n,' Bergman said slowly. 'Our most precious asset - time. The air should last out for thirty hours or so - and we still have freshener cartridges in reserve. I reckon we can sort this out between us, given time.'

Herzog's determination had disintegrated with the discovery that landing on the sub-oceanic ridge was not the solution to their problems. His shoulders slumped and he buried his head in his hands.

'Let's face it, sir. This is the end of the line. We're

only kidding ourselves if we imagine we can get out of this.'

Bergman was near breaking point himself but he kept his nerves under an iron control. 'Well I don't intend to die yet, cox'n,' he said emphatically. 'I've still got a lot of scores to settle and I'm going to make sure I get back so that I can close accounts.'

'What's the use,' Herzog said wearily. 'You've - we've all - done our duty.' He suddenly laughed sardonically. 'I had a score to settle too but I didn't reckon on it happening this way.'

Bergman looked up sharply, every sense alerted by the coxswain's casual remark. If they were going to die anyway ...

'Do you mean me?' he queried.

Herzog nodded. Like the skipper he saw no reason to bandy words at this stage. 'You sank the *Koenig!* The tone of his voice was flat. It was not an accusation. It was a plain and unequivocal statement of fact.

'Is that why you tried to kill me?' Bergman parried. Even now, with death staring him in the face, he was reluctant to admit his guilt.

Herzog, too, shied away from the challenge. He played his next move like a chess master forcing an opponent into an impossible mate.

'My son, Johann, was serving on the *Koenig,*' he said slowly. 'And you made me part of the machine that killed him.'

So that was why. Bergman felt his hands sweating as he read the light of murder in the Coxswain's eyes. They were both at breaking point. The strain of being trapped in the crippled submarine on top of their personal stresses had brought them to the brink of madness. And with death facing them it seemed logical to settle their bitter feud in naked, primeval combat without regard to the lives of the men who now depended on them for survival.

There was a service issue Luger automatic in the top drawer of the bureau and Herzog's eyes followed the *Kapitanleutnant* as he walked towards it. Standing up from the table and kicking the chair aside his massive arms crooked as he crouched forward. Bergman snatched the gun from the half-opened drawer and flicked the safety catch.

'That's far enough, Cox'n.'

The two men glared at each other across the narrow width of the wardroom and Herzog backed away slightly under the threat of the gun in Bergman's hand.

'I was acting under orders when I sank the *Koenig*. I had no alternative. But tell me - were you acting under orders when you betrayed me to the Gestapo? Were you?'

Herzog's back was tight against the bulkhead. He was sweating like a pig and beads of perspiration stood out on his face as he watched the barrel of the Luger move up until it was in line with his navel.

'For Christ's sake come to your senses!'

Von Knebel was easing himself up from the bunk. His face was drawn with pain but, gritting his teeth, he forced himself upright.

'Give me the gun, *Kapitanleutnant*. And you, Coxswain, stand over by the far bulkhead.'

Bergman moved like a man in a dream. He handed the automatic to von Knebel without argument. The Executive Officer's dramatic intervention had drained the anger from his heart and he could feel his body trembling with reaction. Herzog, too, was white-faced and aghast at what he had been about to do. Having reached the precipice, each man withdrew and they stood staring at each other unseeingly.

Von Knebel pushed the gun into his lefthand pocket and motioned them to sit down. 'I suggest that you remember where we are, gentlemen,' he reminded them curtly. 'The lives of forty men depend on your skill and experience. You can kill each other if you want to but not now! Let's get out of this blasted tin coffin first.'

The fever of *blechkoller* had subsided with von Knebel's unexpected intervention and both men stared at each other sheepishly.

'I agree, *Herr Oberleutnant!*' Bergman said stiffly. 'We must think of something - our personal disputes can wait. Some time in the next thirty hours ...'

'Thirty *hours?*'

'That's right, von Knebel,' Bergman confirmed grimly. 'According to my calculations we've got just about thirty hours of air supply left.'

'I doubt if we've even got as much as thirty *minutes'.*' the Executive Officer pointed out sharply. 'Don't you realize we're shipping unstable torpedoes? They could detonate at any minute.'

'How do you know they're unstable?' Bergman frowned. 'You obviously didn't read the memo from DC(T).[1] that turned up just before we left Lorient.'

Bergman shrugged. 'There's too much bloody paperwork at Flotilla - I don't have time to read memos and fill in forms when I'm going out on patrol.'

'In that case I'll tell you what it said. Apparently the *Type G-Ja Mark IIIs* are showing signs of instability. At least two out of every three in service have got a build up of crystals — a deterioration due to old age. DC(T) instructed us to unload any *Mk IIIs* we were carrying in our outfit and replace them with *G-Je's* or one of the later marks. When I went forward to check the bow damage I noticed we were shipping two of the *Mark IIIs* as spares.'

Bergman searched back through his memory and tried to recall the lectures on torpedo maintenance at the Kiel Periscope School. Crystals were a warning sign that the explosive charge in the warhead of the torpedo had deteriorated to the point where the chemicals were unstable and liable to spontaneous detonation. And once in that critical condition no safety devices in the world could stop them from exploding. He shuddered.

'If I remember correctly,' he said slowly, 'excess humidity in the atmosphere makes the condition worse. And if they're in the flooded compartment you can scarcely get more humidity than that.'

Von Knebel nodded. 'Precisely - and that's why I doubt if they'll last more than another thirty minutes.'

Bergman sat down at the table to consider this new threat. To be helplessly trapped inside a crippled U-boat in two hundred feet of water was terrifying enough. But with the probability of two time-bombs likely to explode at any minute. And yet...? Pulling a piece of paper from his pocket he quickly sketched a rough outline of *UB-44*!s cigar-shaped hull. His eyes burned with excitement as he showed it to the others.

'Those two torpedoes could well be the luckiest break we've had so far,' he told them.

Herzog blinked with disbelief. What the hell was the skipper getting at? Von Knebel, fully aware of Bergman's brilliant reputation, took the remark seriously and stared down at the penciled diagram searching for the answer that the skipper had found.

Bergman explained, 'You remember I said that, even

with all tanks blown, a U-boat has insufficient buoyancy to rise to the surface if she has two compartments flooded?'

They nodded. So where does that get us, Herzog wondered.

'Our flooded compartments are in the bows.' Bergman tapped the diagram with his pencil to indicate the location. 'The rest of the boat is watertight and fully buoyant. When those torpedoes go up they'll blow the bow section to smithereens - like this!' His pencil struck at the flooded compartments. 'Now as you can see, all that's left of *UB-44* is the undamaged section from the conning-tower to the stern.'

Von Knebel caught Bergman's excitement as he grasped tire point. 'I see what you mean, sir - with the flooded compartments gone the rest of the boat will be sufficiently buoyant to rise to the surface.' He looked suddenly doubtful. 'But supposing the explosion damages the rest of the boat?'

That's a chance we'll have to take,' Bergman told him cheerfully. 'But as there's no alternative I don't propose to worry about it. If it's any consolation I remember reading about an enemy submarine that ran smack bang into one of our mines and lost her entire bow section. But the watertight bulkheads held and she got back to base in one piece.' He grinned. 'I suppose even half a submarine is better than none.'

'Well if the British can do it there's no reason why we bloody well can't,' Herzog agreed emphatically.

Bergman looked at von Knebel and then at the Coxswain. 'I take it that we are agreed then?'

It was a crazy theory but at least it gave them a straw to cling to in those final hours that linked life with death.

Better to die quickly and cleanly than to spend one's last minutes gasping and choking for breath. They nodded. And they knew that every single man on board *UB-44* would back their decision to the hilt.

Bergman looked at his watch for the twentieth time. The waiting was the worst part. Supposing von Knebel had been wrong about the torpedoes? He glanced across at the Executive Officer to see how he was standing up to the ordeal The *Oberleutnant* was calmly playing poker with Riedel, clutching the cards in the fingers of his splinted right hand, and playing them with his left. Riedel, too, seemed oblivious of any danger and, with his cap tilted back at a rakish angle, he concentrated on his hand as he struggled to out-bluff his experienced opponent.

The watertight door leading through to the flooded sections had been carefully reinforced with stout planks of wood and lengths of bar steel that Herzog had conjured from his secret bosun's store in the bowels of the submarine and sacks of flour, potatoes, and even a dozen hams, had been pressed into use to form a temporary sandbag barrier as protection against steel splinters.

Bergman had also taken the additional precaution of increasing the air pressure inside the boat in an effort to ease the strain on the vital bulkhead. It was a calculated risk for the extra pressure would soon seek out any weak spots in the hull plating and, if they gave way, their last hope of survival would disappear. He cast an anxious eye at the air pressure gauge which Korman had rigged in the control room and was reassured to find it holding steady. Then, unable to resist the temptation, he stole a glance at his watch again. One hour fifty-three minutes.

Bracing his back against the aft bulkhead Bergman

slipped the cuff of his sleeve down to cover his wristwatch and closed his eyes. But his brain continued working unceasingly as he reviewed the firing controls and torpedo circuits in his mind. Several times he thought he had found a method of detonating the warheads from the control room but, on each occasion, and on further examination of the procedures involved, there was always a snag. No — it had to be a spontaneous explosion or nothing. And although he was reluctant to admit it, it seemed likely to be nothing.

Just a slow death after thirty hours of impotently senseless waiting. His thoughts turned to the Luger automatic that von Knebel had replaced in the wardroom locker but he quickly dismissed the idea from his mind. That was the coward's way out. And, whatever else he might be, Bergman was no coward.

UB-44 shook itself like a dog after a swim. There was a sullen roar from the bows and the shrill shriek of rending metal. The entombed men exchanged silent glances as they waited and Bergman unconsciously braced himself more securely as he stared at the watertight door that now stood between him and instant death. It was holding securely without even the slightest trace of leaking. Thank God they knew how to build submarines at the Germania shipyards.

A second and more violent explosion rocked the U-boat bodily, and the men sensed a scraping movement beneath the keel as she lifted from her muddy berth on the midocean ridge. The stern rose slightly placing *UB-44* in an odd tail-up attitude and sweating hands gripped their supports more firmly to maintain balance.

'She's rising!'

Herzog pointed excitedly at the depth-gauge and

Bergman got up from his position on the floor to check. She was certainly lifting. But slowly - too slowly. He suspected that the ballast tanks had been damaged by the explosion and the soft gurgle of water echoing inside the hull confirmed his thoughts.

'Blow all tanks ! And keep blowing.' As Maas and Shoe mann hurried to turn the blowing valves Bergman picked up the telephone to the engine room. 'Any sign of flooding aft?' 'No, sir. The hull's as tight as a duck's arse.'

'Open all watertight doors and start coming forward to the control room. And keep them well spaced out, Korman. I don't want to upset the trim.'

Von Knebel had joined him at the diving table. He watched the flickering needles of the pressure gauges as the air hissed into the damaged tanks and then moved on to check the depth indicators.

'We're going up faster now, sir.'

'So far,' Bergman warned quietly, 'but both six and eight tanks seem to be holed. If we run out of air they'll flood within seconds and take us straight back to the bottom again. It's still touch and go.'

'Forty feet and rising.'

'Thirty feet and rising.'

'Open the lower hatch, Riedel. And hang on tight - the extra air pressure will blow you clean out the boat if you're not careful.' He picked up the microphone and held it close to his mouth. 'All hands prepare to abandon ship. All hands prepare to abandon ship.' Suddenly, out of the corner of his eye, Bergman saw one of the pressure gauge needles fall away. 'Maas! By-pass the line to Number Six! Get some more air into that bloody tank or we'll go down!'

Herzog picked up a spanner and joined in the

struggle to shut off the pressure and link in the alternative air line. *UB-44's* sudden ascent faltered and she seemed to hang motionless in the water - precariously balanced between the surface and the sea bottom like an aquatic puppet on a string. The buzzer of the telephone sounded and von Knebel picked up the instrument.

'It's Korman, sir. The door out of the motor room is jammed and they can't get it open. The blast must have been playing tricks and buckled the seating.'

'Tell them to keep trying.'

'Ten feet, sir!'

'Open the upper hatch - up you go. *Raus, raus!* At the double.'

The sweet tang of salt fresh air filled the control room and Bergman drew a deep breath into his lungs as the men followed each other up the narrow ladder into the conning-tower. It was good to be alive.

A violent crack of ripping metal and the angry roar of water emphasized how close he had been to death. The damaged ballast tank had suddenly collapsed and *UB-44* was flooding again. Swinging round, he thrust von Knebel towards the ladder.

'Hurry, man. Hurry!'

Even as he spoke, the U-boat began to tilt crazily to starboard in readiness for her final plunge to the bottom.

'But the men in the stern, sir,' von Knebel protested. 'The door's still jammed ..

Bergman knew there was no hope. *UB-44* was going down fast and even the slightest delay would be fatal. And having come so far he had no intention of dying now.

'Leave them!' he shouted at the Executive Officer. 'They can't get out now. Save yourself, for God's sake!'

But the *Oberleutnant* ignored the order. Stepping

down from the ladder he ducked through the watertight door swinging freely from its hinges at the rear of the control room and set off grimly towards the jammed hatch that sealed off the motor room and the stern compartments. Thirty men were still trapped behind that steel wall and he had to try and do something.

UB-44 lurched more steeply and Bergman knew she was beginning to slide back beneath the surface. Steeling himself to the fate of the men entombed in the stern compartments, he grabbed the rungs of the ladder and hauled himself up towards the sunlight streaming down through the open hatch. And, as he climbed to safety, he could hear von Knebel hammering vainly at the jammed lock of the motor room door deep down inside the hull.

Bergman's feelings were mixed as *UB-44.* sank beneath his feet - gratitude that he was still alive, regret that his boat had gone, and fear of what the future held. For now he was naked in the face of his enemies. The Fuehrer's signal ordering him to sink the *Koenig* still lay locked inside the U- boat's safe - two hundred feet below on the bottom of the ocean. And without the signal as evidence he had no defence against the charge of murdering a thousand German sailors.

Treading water and spitting the sea from his mouth Bergman reflected on his inevitable fate if Gorst ever learned the truth of the *Koenig* incident. Until now the secret had seemed secure and he had retained the Fuehrer's signal as a possible weapon to use against the dictator when the time was ripe to overthrow him. But now, as he had discovered within the last few hours, Herzog also shared the fatal knowledge that *UB-44* had been responsible for the *Koenig's* destruction.

A strong arm circled his shoulders to drag him clear of

the suction created by the sinking submarine and he heard Herzog's voice in his ear.

'Take it easy, sir, you're okay now.'

Bergman spat out another mouthful of oil-scummed water and began swimming towards *UB-44*'s rubber dinghy which someone had miraculously released. The Coxswain swam watchfully at his side.

'Drache managed to get a radio signal off before he got out, sir. There should be another U-boat in the area to pick us up in a couple of hours.'

Bergman nodded, snatched a quick breath of air into his lungs, and fumbled for the clasp-knife hooked to his belt. His head went under as he used both hands to open the blade and he emerged gasping and spluttering.

'Pity about the others,' Herzog was saying. 'But that's the way it goes. It's no use being sentimental when you're serving in U-boats.'

Bergman grasped the knife tightly in his right hand. The dinghy was barely ten yards away. This was the only chance he had. The blade drove upwards with all his strength behind it and he felt it grate against the Coxswain's ribs as it sank home. Herzog threshed the water like a wounded whale and his lips parted in a rictus of pain as if he was grinning in triumph. The knife stabbed into his body again and, rolling over, he floated face down in the sea.

Bergman let the murder weapon sink to the bottom and struck out strongly for the dinghy. Maas and Schoemann reached over to help him and, grasping their hands, he allowed his body to go limp as they dragged him to safety.

Neither of the men had seen the last grim act of the drama and Bergman shivered with reaction as he sprawled in the bottom of the dinghy retching up sea-water and gasping for breath. The secret of the *Koenig* affair was safe once more. But at what a price. He closed his eyes and gathered his thoughts.

There had been a certain bitter irony in Herzog's last words. In fact the coxswain might almost have been writing his own epitaph.

'There is no room for sentiment in a U-boat.'

Perhaps he should have added - when *Kapitanleut-nant* Bergman is in command.

UB-44 (Type VIIB - modified)

    Builders: Germania Werft (Kiel).

    Completed: 17 October 1938.

    Length: 218 feet 3 inches.

    Beam: 20 feet 3 inches.

    Draught: 15 feet 6 inches.

    Machinery: Two shaft MAN diesel engines of 2,800 BHP Electric motors of 750 SHP.

    Displacement: 753 tons (Surface) 857 tons (Submerged).

    Speed: 17J knots (Surface), 8 knots (Submerged).

    Bunkers: 108 tons oil fuel.

    Range: 6,500 miles @ 12 knots (Surface).

    80 miles @ 4 knots (Submerged).

    Armament: One 88mm (3'5''/) [35] designed. Replaced by one 105mm (4-1'') in early 1940.

    One 20mm AA.

    Five 533mm torpedo tubes (Four bows, one stern).

    Twelve torpedoes carried.

    Complement: 44.

Author's Note: There were various crew changes after every patrol and these have not been fully covered in the text. Unfortunately the personnel records of the 10th Flotilla were destroyed during an air raid on Wilhelmshaven in April 1944 and accurate details are therefore not available.

A LOOK AT: TOKYO TORPEDO (BOOK THREE IN THE U-BOAT SERIES)

During the terrible Battle of the Atlantic, Hitler's U-Boats had become the scourge of the ocean. Of all of his U-Boat aces, none as more brilliant or more feared than Kapitanleutnant Konrad Bergman.

But while Bergman had been prowling the Atlantic convoy routes, another deadly conflict was raging under burning Eastern skies. When word came that Japan and invented a weapon that could swing the pendulum of the war for Germany, it was Bergman who was sent to slip through the American net and wrest the secret of the Tokyo Torpedo from Japan—single-handed!

AVAILABLE SEPTEMBER 2018 FROM EDWYN GRAY AND WOLFPACK PUBLISHING

ABOUT THE AUTHOR

AUTHOR EDWIN GRAY specialized in naval writing, and has occasionally written short stories.

Born in London, Gray pursued his education at the Royal Grammar School, High Wycombe. After reading economics at the University of London, he went on to join the British civil service.

Gray began his career as an author in 1953, writing for magazines. His first novel was published in 1969, and he became a full-time writer in 1980.